Convicted

A. Michele Henderson

Ardena Henderson Publishing

Dedication

    I dedicate this book to my readers. Thank you for the emails, inboxes and comments. Just when I think my stories aren't making an impact, one of you will share with me how my books have touched your life. Your loyalty and expectation inspire me to push my pen into those hard places concerning the human experience. Thank you for traveling this road with me I couldn't do this without you.

Acknowledgements

Giving all honor and glory to my Heavenly Father who enables me through His Spirit to walk in purpose. To my husband James for your unwavering love. I am grateful for the life we've built together and I honor God for blessing me with you. To our son Joshua who motivates me to be a better person each day, I love you. To our family, pastors, church family, mentors and supporters I love and appreciate you all. To the awesome women who I call my sisters and friends, I cannot express how much you all mean to me. We are proof that women can coexist in harmony without competition, comparison or confusion. I love you all.

Special Thanks

To my husband James for managing the business side of my endeavors, I couldn't do this without you. To Candice my special events manager extraordinaire, you are the bomb.com honey (in your voice). To my administrator LaKesha, for keeping things in order and on time, thank you Sis. To Ricky Alston for your specialized expertise, thank you. To my confidantes who keep me in the game, you know who you are xoxo.

Table of Contents

amichelehenderson.com

Disclaimer: The storyline of this novel is a work of fiction and does not depict the lives of actual persons. Real life locations and pop culture icons are used for context and relatability. The author reserves the right to reference herself as a writing signature.

Chapter 1: Crime Star

*T*HE burning sensation of ammonia gas in Sydney's nostrils, jolted her back into consciousness. When she came to herself, she could feel sharp pains in the back of her head from falling to the floor. As the paramedics placed her on the gurney she realized that she was still in the courtroom. The rumble of the crowd caused her stomach to knot and she became nauseous. As she was wheeled out of the courtroom she began to vomit. Just then a photographer captured the image that would travel halfway around the world. Sydney Marie Kane fainted and fell to the floor after a jury of her peers, convicted her of second degree murder. She looked at the crowd and saw her boyfriend Danny who looked at her in disbelief. Kent and Linda turned away as if they had no part in her shame. Absent was her mother Shelby who was raising her two children back home in Oklahoma; since she ran off to Las Vegas for a "better life." She saw Leslie and Savannah look upon her with disdain along with Judy Abal, Milla's mom. Her heart sank into her stomach and terror encompassed her. Sydney's future was uncertain and prison was the last place on earth she ever wanted to be. She was only 26 years old, yet life as she knew it was over.

A. Michele Henderson

Six weeks later, on a thundering Thursday morning, Sydney stood before a judge to be sentenced. Milla's mother Judy, her fiancé Malcom and kid sister Morgan all read statements to the judge about what kind of woman she was, before Sydney's actions stole her young life. Milla's father Joe was so overcome with emotion he couldn't read his statement and instead broke down in tears. Sydney never looked at them directly and was moved by Joe's agony. She hadn't ever met her father and envied Milla for having such a great dad. She relived that day over and over in her mind and wished she could take it back. Lost in her thoughts of shame and regret for taking someone's life and never being able to be a mother to her children, Sydney began to cry. After all the character statements were read, the judge told Sydney and her attorney to stand. With a stern look on his face, judge Michael A. Wilkins sentenced Sydney to 25 years in prison without the possibility of parole. Loud cries and cheers could be heard in the courtroom. Sydney's entire body became numb. In utter disbelief, Milla's parents yelled out obscenities because they wanted a harsher sentence. The judge had already considered their pain and removed the possibility of parole after 10 years but in the state of Nevada, 25 years was the maximum sentence for murder in the second degree. As the judge called for order, Sydney knew she was on her own. Danny didn't show up nor did Leslie and Savannah. Her attorney had spoken to her mother and relayed the message that she could write and call the children but Shelby had no intention of bringing them on prison visits. After sentencing, her attorney Liam told her that due to the high-profile nature of the case she would spend her first ninety days in Indiana but would serve the remainder of her sentence at the Chesapeake Detention Facility in Baltimore, Maryland.

Unlike the Hollywood film Sydney's extradition was not on Con Air. She was transferred by a red eye commercial flight to begin her sentence in Indiana. She hadn't eaten much in weeks and cried every night. Her emaciated body weighed only 90 pounds and her hair was shedding rapidly. Gone was the glamorous girl who dared to be famous. She was kept alone in a cell and spent her first night rocking back and forth. During the night, she looked at the ceiling thinking about how she ended up in such a horrible pit.

Five Years Earlier

Sydney struggled to get the front door of her trailer unlocked while carrying Jill and her laundry. She plopped Jill on the couch and sat the laundry bags on the floor. Her back ached and her feet were swollen after working a ten hour shift. The upside to waitressing at Ruby's Diner was being able to bring food home whenever she wanted, so keeping hot meals on the table, were the easiest tasks of her day. Sydney glanced at the calendar and realized she had a doctor's appointment the following afternoon. She was 8 months pregnant with her second child by Larry who she hadn't seen since he left for work on Friday morning. As usual last Friday was his payday and he was somewhere gambling and drinking it all away. Sydney told Larry she was moving back home with her mother Shelby if he didn't change. Thankfully she had her own car but she wasn't enthused about taking care of another child by herself. She thought about her life as she put the laundry away. She was only 21 and with two children and no high school diploma, she felt stuck. Sydney wished she had stayed in high school and dated Brad Johnson. He liked her all through middle school but she thought he was too straight laced. His grandfather was a preacher and his family were devout Christians who were well known throughout Tulsa. She remembered him telling her as a teen that he was saving his virginity for his wife. Even though he was widely popular and a star athlete he never yielded to peer pressure and wouldn't drink or party. Instead he would take a stand for his faith and invited friends to church. He even invited Sydney who would always make an excuse for why she was unable to go. Just last week, Sydney overheard his mother telling Ruby that he was a junior in college studying to be a doctor. He'd made it all the way to New York. How could she be so foolish? Instead of enjoying her teens, Sydney began sneaking into bars a few towns over with her best friend Jillian. They partied, smoked and dated older men. Not long afterwards they stopped going to school and got jobs. That's when Sydney started dating Larry, who was eight years her senior. At the age of 17 Sydney became pregnant with her daughter who she named after her best friend. Everyone thought she and Larry were married because they shared the same last name. After the first few months of dating they found out that Larry's father had been adopted by Sydney's great uncle but they weren't blood related. Jillian decided to "grow up" and returned to school. Sydney admired Jill for going back to high school instead of getting her G.E.D but she was too embarrassed to start from scratch at the age where she should've been graduating. After graduation Jillian went to junior college before transferring to Northeastern State University where she earned her B.S.N. Over time they lost touch and Jillian moved on to bigger and better things. Sydney knew from Jillian's brother Pete that she was working at a hospital in Oklahoma City. Even though it was just an hour and a half away Sydney had never been that far outside of Tulsa. She always wanted to reconnect with Jillian but no longer felt good enough to be in her life. She tried connecting with her once on social media but Jill never accepted her request.

Seven full days after her due date, Sydney pushed while holding her mother's hand on a rainy April morning. After 3 hours of labor she gave birth to a healthy baby boy. She named him Richard after her grandfather and Colby after her favorite cheese. Richard Colby Kane was 6lbs 6oz with a head full of curly auburn locks, just like his mother. She hadn't seen Larry in over three weeks since moving out to live with her mom but she hoped he would come to the hospital.

In less than a month, Sydney was back down to her pre-baby weight of 142 pounds. She returned to work the following week after finding childcare that fit her budget. One evening while picking Richie up from daycare, his caregiver Susan was watching a reality television show. A group of women in Florida were on the show shopping and partying. Sydney couldn't believe people could get money for having fun. Susan told her who the women were and the premise of the show. She drank it in as if it were nourishing to her soul and wanted to get satellite television so she could watch too. The women looked so happy, glamorous and carefree. They had perfect looks, beautiful clothes and were everything Sydney wanted to be.

The following morning at work Sydney was serving the regulars at the diner while daydreaming about having a new life. She could take twenty patron's orders without writing them down because they ate the same thing every single day. She wanted to be like Britney Joseph, the star of Glam Wives. She lived in a big house, drove a convertible like Barbie™, had a house keeper and shopped daily. Sydney imagined herself as Britney and decided she would act like her for the remainder of her shift. She smiled like Britney, walked liked Britney and talked like Britney. The regulars were quite amused. Ruby noticed the new Sydney and shook her head. The customers were happy and she had a smile on her face, so Ruby considered it customer service. After all being goofy wasn't a crime and it was surely better than post-partum depression.

During the lunch shift Sydney almost dropped everyone's drinks when she overheard a group of women talking about the show. Some of them liked Britney but most of them liked Scarlett. Sydney took mental notes while the college friends talked. They said Scarlett was prettier because she had breast implants, lip injections and was way skinnier. They all agreed that Britney dressed the best and tanned much better. The ladies discussed their trip to Miami where the show was taped and all they planned to do while there. One of the girls said she'd rather go to Vegas because whatever happens there, stays there. The group erupted into laughter and gave each other high fives. Sydney envied them for being able to travel. She also envied them for going to college. She thought about how different her life would've been had she made different choices. One of the girls at the table was Taylor Wyatt. When she and Sydney were in the 8th grade, all the boys liked her. She looked much different now with full lips, tanned skin and huge breast implants. As if Taylor had just noticed her when the check came she asked if Sydney was the same Sydney Kane who went to school with her. Sydney admitted that it was her and Taylor offered Sydney her phone number so they could catch up.

For weeks Sydney was too ashamed of her life to call Taylor. She thought she wasn't smart or pretty enough; to hang around Taylor and her college friends. One night after a few drinks with Shelby and re-watching every episode of Glam Wives, she decided to reach out to Taylor. When Taylor answered, she was excited to hear from her. The two schoolmates talked on the phone for over six hours. Sydney learned that Taylor had a daughter with Jason Bixby who was the popular boy in 8th grade. They dated in high school and planned to go to college together. During 11th grade she became pregnant and their relationship fell apart. The two high school sweethearts went their separate ways but co parented their child. Jason was now married to her ex best friend Kelly and had full custody of their daughter Jewel. Taylor told Sydney that Jason was granted custody because he was married and had a good job. Sydney shared her woes with Taylor before finding out she was staying in a Las Vegas penthouse as they spoke. Taylor told Sydney she was living with her boyfriend Dale who managed a Las Vegas nightclub. She told Sydney that she hadn't been to class in months but kept up the college girl façade for her family. One of her friends taught her the game of getting and keeping influential men for her own personal gain. Taylor told Sydney that influential men loved trophy girlfriends and wives and if she was willing to play the game, she would teach her how. She offered to introduce Sydney to Dale's brother Danny who was a pit boss at the same hotel's casino. Without hesitation Sydney agreed but Taylor told Sydney she had to be fixed up first. Sydney didn't know all that it entailed but she was willing to do anything to become anyone but herself.

Chapter 2: The Persian Princess

SYDNEY sat beside Taylor in first class on edge. She downed her third scotch to calm her nerves. She'd never flown before and was extremely nervous. Taylor was cool as a cucumber along with the other passengers in the cabin. Sydney had taken a leave of absence from Ruby's and Taylor gave Shelby $2500 to look after Sydney's children. Shelby hadn't seen that kind of money since 1974 so it was her pleasure. Sydney told her mom the truth about where she was going and why. With her mother's blessing, Sydney boarded the flight to Miami for a full body makeover.

Sydney couldn't believe her eyes when they drove up Collins Avenue. It was a hot July afternoon and beautiful people were everywhere. Taylor pulled the car into a multilevel garage and rode up to her private parking spot. When she opened the door to her condominium Sydney gasped at the floor to ceiling views of the Miami shoreline. Taylor showed her to the guest room so she could unpack. When she looked over the bedroom and attached on-suite, Sydney was blown away. She'd never slept in a king size bed or bathed in a tub so deep. Taylor had the same bath products as Britney from Glam Wives. She didn't know who Jo Malone was but she couldn't wait to soak in his bath oil and slather her body with his lotion. Taylor also had the shampoo, conditioner and ginormous candles. That evening the ladies stayed in and ate takeout from Zuma. Taylor taught Sydney that the quickest way to be detected as a fraud was to have an unsophisticated palate. Sydney had never eaten Japanese and thoroughly enjoyed the meal. Taylor instructed her never to order burgers or chicken of any kind. That night, Taylor laid out the dos and don'ts of the "trophy wife life." Tomorrow, after a light breakfast, the ladies would go to Sydney's consultation for breast augmentation, liposuction and a Brazilian butt lift. Once she was healed she would also get dental veneers, lip injections, a new hair color, extensions and a spray tan. Once her makeover was complete, Taylor would take her shopping for her sin city debut. Sydney could hardly sleep that night. She was in the same city as Britney. She wondered how far Taylor's condo was from Britney's house and how much fun she must've been having. Little did Sydney know, Britney Joseph had flown to Cambridge, Massachusetts to visit her grandparents.

The following morning Sydney was nervous during her consultation. She'd only been nude in front of Larry and it felt awkward to have a stranger stare at her body. The plastic surgeon took measurements and drew on her with a marker as if her nudity meant nothing. Taylor knew all the lingo and discussed the procedure with "Dr. Bling." The doctor approved the surgery and the appointment was booked. Sydney was all in after watching Taylor pay for her $18,000.00 surgery, with one swipe of a card. Sydney became overwhelmed with emotion because Taylor was willing to help her, using her own money.

Ten weeks later after a few complications, Sydney stepped off the plane in Las Vegas with straightened raven locks, full lips, a 20-inch waist and a double D bra. Donned in a tangerine Hervé Leger bandage dress and Aquazzura sandals, Sydney turned heads. The boost that plastic surgery gave to her confidence, made her feel like a million bucks. When they arrived at the hotel the limo driver and doorman treated the ladies like royalty. Sydney wasn't accustomed to so much attention but she was beginning to enjoy it. Taylor walked Sydney to her room before rushing to her and Dale's suite, since she hadn't seen him in months. Just when Sydney began to unpack there was a knock at the door. It was Danny coming to introduce himself and inspect her. Danny was floored by how beautiful she was and asked if she was Persian. She lied and said her father was and Danny was pleased. He told her not to unpack and to follow him to his suite. He said he wasn't sure if she'd be ugly in which case he would've sent her home. Sydney wasn't offended that Danny wouldn't have found her attractive before the surgery and decided to play a role, just like an actress.

Within a few weeks, Sydney started sending money to Shelby for her and the children. Danny got her a job as a cocktail waitress on the high roller's floor and with her paycheck, tips and the money he gave her; she was clearing $15k a month. By the end of the year she had paid Taylor back with interest and became the "it" girl, on her own. Still channeling her inner "Britney", Sydney created an entirely new persona in her mind. It wasn't long before she lost touch with reality and immersed herself into the life she'd created. She would often receive extravagant gifts from the whales, while shopping for their wives during the day. They came from all over the world to gamble and often came with shopping lists of things their wives, daughters and girlfriends wanted. Personal shopping acquainted Sydney with designer labels and current trends in fashion. Back in Tulsa she had no idea that a luxury community existed. Spending thousands of dollars on goods and services woke up a monster inside of Sydney. Coming into the knowledge of all the things she'd been deprived of, made her greedy. Seduced by the glitter and glamour caused her to make inner vows. Sydney refused to be broke, average or wanting another day in her life.

One morning on the casino floor, Sydney thought about Larry. It was his dream to win big but it never happened. He had gambled their bill money away so many times and became an alcoholic by medicating his losses. These men had professions and gambled for sport. There were some gambling addicts on the main floor but they never reached the status of a whale. These men would lose millions and never bat an eye. It amazed Sydney how great the gulf was between the rich and the poor, the haves and the have nots. She learned over time that poverty wasn't just the lack of finances but the absence of information. Most of what the gamblers spoke about went over her head. She knew she was positioned to learn things the average person would never be exposed to but her level of comprehension was low. Many of her co-workers had established profitable businesses just from the knowledge gained from overheard conversations. Sydney hoped that she could learn something that would change her life forever but for now, she'd remain their go-to shopper.

As time passed, Sydney fell in love with Danny and was no longer acting. She wanted a future with him but was afraid to tell him about Jill and Richie. By the two year mark, she had a six-figure nest egg and was sending her mother $5k each month. The last time she spoke to her mother, Shelby had moved out of her trailer and into a 3 bedroom cottage, with the kids. Larry was in jail for DUI and had been fired from his job. On her 23rd birthday Dale threw Sydney a party at the club. She was placed on flyers and complete strangers came to party with her. Celebrities showed up including her favorite singer Nino. He dedicated songs to her and invited her on stage to sing. She and her new best friend Leslie danced for hours. Before the night was over Danny presented her with a cake made like her favorite designer handbag. As if Nino wasn't the best surprise ever, Danny took her outside and presented her with a 7 series BMW custom painted to be the exact match of her favorite Kat Von D liquid lipstick, L.U.V. Sydney couldn't believe how great her life had become and celebrated her new found acceptance.

Sydney befriended Leslie, who lived in Las Vegas with her fiancé Lloyd. Lloyd was the current heavyweight champion of the world. Women who didn't even know Leslie hated her just because she was with him. They were a flashy couple who both had loads of style. He spoiled her with exotic gifts and trips. The two women had a lot in common and both had undergone plastic surgery to be on a powerful man's arm. Unlike Danny, Lloyd knew Leslie grew up in the projects of St Louis and paid for her surgery. She appreciated Leslie for knowing the truth and still accepting her. They guarded each other's secrets and were very close. Each month they'd get together to eat ramen noodles and drink tang. It was their version of paying homage to the lives they left behind. They both knew what it was like to improvise with a little bit of money and enjoyed each other's company. Sydney never had a black friend and was surprised by how much broke people had in common regardless of color. Leslie taught Sydney how to make collard greens and Sydney introduced Leslie to green bean casserole. The two friends often took trips together on Lloyd's private jet. Together they'd already gone to Mexico, Hawaii, Puerto Rico and Anguilla. Leslie introduced her to high end designer labels and bought Sydney her first Birkin bag. Because of who Lloyd was, Leslie never had to play the waiting list game and could walk in any store and leave with what she wanted. The two friends lived a lavish life. They drank cocktails with diamonds in the bottom of their glasses and ate burgers with 18kt gold on them. They would document their shopping excursions on social media and cause an uproar with their excessive spending. On one occasion their lives were threatened for burning what their audience believed to be $50,000. They had panned the camera away and replaced the real money with play money but it sent social media into a frenzy. All the viewers saw, were $100s and $50s on fire and the masses were livid. The two friends were amused by the complete strangers who'd get upset over what they had and did. Every time they were together they had loads of fun. They dubbed themselves Thelma and Louise and caused a stir everywhere they went. The two women also caught the attention of who they dubbed as haters for the way they dressed. Showing off their naturally unattainable figures, the two women often wore lingerie as outfits. They both had come a long way from the trailer park and the projects and celebrated themselves daily.

One evening while Sydney was serving the baccarat table, one of the casino regulars introduced her to Kent Johnson. He and his partner Linda Casey were the producers of the hit reality shows, Glam Wives and Football Fiancés. Sydney couldn't believe her ears. Kent told her they were interested in making a Las Vegas version of their popular shows and would call it Casino Wives. Sydney told them she was interested and agreed to meet with Kent and Linda the following evening.

During the meeting, Kent and Linda pitched the show and asked who Sydney thought would like to be a part of it. She suggested Leslie and Taylor. A week later both women signed on and Taylor suggested Savannah, who was the legal wife of a hotel mogul. Days later they scouted Milla who owned a successful boutique at the Atlantis underwater hotel. Milla was engaged to Malcom Ross the current MVP of the NBA championship team, the Las Vegas Dice. The ladies had a screen test to determine chemistry and diversity. Savannah was the eldest at 30 and Leslie was the youngest at 22. Each woman was given a contract for $50k but were promised more if the show became a hit. Savannah planned on using the platform to bring awareness to the plight of women in her native country, Milla wanted to use the platform to promote her boutique, Leslie wanted to use her platform to bring awareness to police brutality among people of color, Taylor wanted to promote her new makeup line and Sydney wanted to be famous!

A. Michele Henderson

Each woman being armed with personal ideals and goals allowed the cameras to document their lives. Savannah, Leslie and Milla were careful of the images they portrayed for all to see. Somewhat holding back in the name of tact and decency the three women considered their families and communities during the filming process. Sydney and Taylor however were two horses of a different color. Each competing to be the lead, allowed the cameras to magnify their dysfunction and perpetuate their ignorance. After three months of taping, Casino Wives was set to premier. Kent and Linda told the ladies to enjoy their last few days of obscurity because their lives would change forever. They warned the ladies that their lives would no longer be their own and wished them great success. While the women considered what fame would mean for them and their families, Sydney could care less. Now was the time to prove she was no longer the teen mom who was destined for a life of mediocrity. Men did double takes when she walked by and women wanted to be her. Fame would just mean adoration on another level! She would get back at Jillian for leaving her and show Brad what he was missing. Sydney was about to be a star.

To prepare for the red carpet premier the following evening, Sydney checked into the spa. After a fresh dye job and new haircut with layers she was whisked off to lunch before a hot stone massage, manicure and pedicure. During lunch, she made small talk with a woman named Ardena. She was on vacation with her husband and was relaxing before the new Cirque du Soleil show. Ardena had a confidence about her that Sydney couldn't place. After a few minutes of small talk, she recognized It as the same confidence that rested on Brad. Whatever it was or however she got it, she wore it well.It was premier night and the watch party was in full swing. In support of Kent and Linda's new venture all the women of their previous shows came out to support. The new cast was cordial to the veterans but had no intention of perpetuating their level of ignorance over the airwaves. Both of Kent and Linda's previous shows were earmarked by violent outbursts and FCC violations. Due to a legal filing Football Fiancés was cancelled. Sydney was so excited to meet Britney that she fumbled her words. She spent over an hour telling Britney how great she was and how she inspired her to take charge of her life. To Sydney's surprise Britney was a graduate of Stanford Law and had earned her Juris Doctor at just 22 years old. Sydney asked her why the show doesn't feature her as an attorney and Britney told her it would jeopardize her legitimacy in the legal world. "You have to remember this business isn't real. They're hiring you to push an agenda." Britney stated. "If people watched me prepare briefs and consult prospective clients they would fall asleep", Britney laughed. Sydney was disappointed that the woman she based her entire persona on, was also just playing a role. Scarlett made her more comfortable because she came from a troubled background and didn't graduate high school. Educated women made Sydney uncomfortable because they always seemed to look down on her.

Across the room at the punch bowl Milla was introduced to Brooke Taylor who stared on Football Fiancés. By the end of the premier they decided to exchange numbers and keep in touch. Milla listened as Brooke filled her in on the 180° turn her life took after the show was cancelled. She also learned that Brooke was living in Northern Virginia and owned a successful shoe boutique. They agreed to work together as Milla specialized in apparel and Brooke specialized in footwear. The guests at the premier were treated to the first 2 of 12 episodes and gave great feedback about what they saw. Each woman was depicted as a playing card in the opening credits. Savannah was the queen because she was the eldest of the bunch, Sydney was an ace, Taylor was the joker, Leslie was the heart of the show and Milla was the diamond.

Savannah Chand

Savannah grew up in Kentucky with her mother and grandmother when they had the opportunity to leave Nepal. With only the ability to take one of her children Savannah's mother chose her, being the youngest. In the hope for Savannah to have a better life and an education, she was renamed at the age of three but was born with the name Bishala. Armed with a formal education and an opportunity to succeed, Savannah graduated at the top of her class in elementary, middle and high school. She was her class valedictorian in undergrad and her class Salutatorian in grad school. After earning two business degrees from Columbia, Savannah quickly rose on the Manhattan corporate scene. With a focus on mergers and acquisitions Savannah was well known as a fierce negotiator among her colleagues. During a business trip to London she met Mithush Chand a Nepali hotel mogul. Shortly after marriage they settled in New York and started a family. Just last year Mithush discovered the opportunity of a lifetime when a Las Vegas hotel was struggling. With Savannah as his secret weapon they acquired a struggling hotel and transformed it into a Las Vegas hot spot. With the support of her husband and three young children, Savannah used the Casino Wives platform to shed light on Nepal's refusal to educate girls.

Milla Abal

Milla grew up in the Mission Hills area of San Diego, California. As the biracial daughter of Judy and Joseph Abal she often struggled to find a place among her peers. Her younger sister Morgan was darker than her and found it easier to fit in and relate to other black girls. Milla on the other hand didn't assimilate as well. People who didn't know Milla accused her of having work done when they saw her full lips and curvy body. Her light complexion and long black hair were juxtaposed to her ethnic features. Milla suffered from seasons of depression because of the rejection she received from both of her racial groups. She was picked on mercilessly and by her sophomore year in high school, Joe allowed her to be homeschooled. During her freshman year, she began dating Malcolm Ross, the star of the varsity basketball team. Because of homeschooling Milla graduated a year early and began to attend college for fashion merchandising and business. After graduation, she and Malcolm moved to Las Vegas when he was drafted by his current team. Though their relationship looks great from the outside, Malcolm isn't the model fiancé. He's had two children by two other women and his cheating ways are at an all-time high. Since his notoriety has increased, Malcolm has been hard to live with and impossible to trust. Before opening her boutique, Milla spent her days and nights by the phone and stalking other women on social media. She wished she was more like Morgan and knew her worth to walk away. Instead she blames herself for

Malcolm's cruel treatment and pretends as if everything is fine. Each day a part of her dies as Malcolm grows more distant. His behavior has caused Milla to doubt her womanhood and her self-esteem is at an all-time low.

Casino Wives became an overnight sensation and garnered daily entertainment news coverage. Over the next few months the ladies appeared on radio shows, television shows and celebrity versions of game shows. As their popularity grew so did the scrutiny upon their lives. Before they began taping for season two each lady was caught up in the gossip mill. Savannah was accused of being an illegal immigrant when a family member took money in exchange for a false story. After months of backlash Savannah's legal documentation was displayed on a national morning show. The ugly side of fame began to rear its ugly head and there was no turning back. Leslie came under fire when her mother got caught writing bad checks and people accused her of living the high life while her mother remained in poverty. The truth was, Leslie hadn't seen her mother since the age of five when social services removed her and her siblings from her mother's care. The children were found in horrific conditions without food, electricity or heat. The roach infested public housing unit was filthy. The five children under the age of 7 were eating out of the trash and drinking spoiled milk. The authorities discovered their sub human conditions after Leslie's brother was rushed to the hospital, from the expired food they consumed daily. After a few months in foster care an older cousin stepped in to raise her. The public didn't care, all they could see was what they wanted to see. Complete strangers would attack her on social media and bloggers began to spread untruths.

Lloyd and Leslie's lavish lifestyle came under fire by the very media outlets that praised Lloyd's success. Taylor was no stranger to controversy but became humiliated when Jason appeared on Edition Inside to tell the world how he and his wife had to take custody of Jewel when they discovered her eating cat food out of the family pet's bowl. Taylor was passed out on the kitchen floor and couldn't remember the last time the child had been fed. With no diaper on and wearing the same dress for at least a week, Jason quickly took his neglected toddler and filed charges against Taylor. Surprisingly Taylor was a crystal meth addict and was charged with endangerment of a minor at just 18 years old. Real court documents were plastered all over the internet and Taylor's story was true. The entire cast began to look differently at Taylor and she became the looser of the bunch. Milla's embarrassment was placed on the largest platform when Malcolm's two secret children were discovered. The women published text messages and released private conversations between them and Malcolm. Milla gave him her ring back and moved out of his mansion. The public began to accost her on social media calling her stupid and dumb. She became the punch line of jokes for late night comedians. Milla's boutique began to receive prank calls and she was forced to hire an employee to screen them. A couple women would send her pictures of them with Malcolm and then appear on gossip shows. Milla felt so alone and abandoned and it was Brooke's friendship that kept her afloat. Somehow Sydney's past didn't show up in the media but she was accused of being a prostitute. Men would lie on any platform given to them that she was more than a waitress. Instead of destroying her image the public supported her and called evil good.

A. Michele Henderson

She became a spokeswoman for adult products and the face of a dating website. Sydney loved the attention and thought there was no such thing as bad publicity.

Chapter 3: Dancing With the Devil

OF the entire cast, Milla was the most sensitive. The humiliation she endured as Malcolm's girlfriend and fiancée had all but destroyed her. It was just a week before the stories broke, that she called Morgan in tears about Malcolm's slithering ways. Though Morgan was younger, Milla valued her opinion. Just like she had for the past two years, Morgan told Milla to leave him. Morgan didn't see the point in Milla holding on if she was so miserable. In contrast when Milla cried to her mother Judy about Malcolm's infidelity, Judy told her to stick it out. "Look Milla, men aren't exactly breaking down the door to be with you," said Judy. "Sometimes you have to accept the part of a man that he's willing to give you" Judy said in a dismissing tone. "Do you know why I married your father? Because he was the first man who asked" Judy said dryly. Milla sobbed as she listened, always assuming her parents were in love. Why else would a black woman endure the scrutiny of marrying a white man whose family didn't accept her? Milla thought to herself. Judy's advice confused Milla even more. The pain was becoming unbearable and she needed sleeping pills to fall asleep at night and antidepressants to keep her functional during the day. She contemplated suicide daily and found it nearly impossible to smile. Her therapy sessions with Dr. Bryant had gone from twice a month to five days per week. She had no rest for her weary soul and was tormented in her mind daily. Outwardly nobody noticed a thing. The ladies of the cast were too caught up in her sense of style and quiet demeanor. Sydney especially envied Milla because her style was impeccable. Sydney would spend days planning her outfits only for Milla to walk in the room and receive all the compliments. She was dying inside right before their eyes and nobody noticed a thing.

A week had gone by since Malcolm's dirty laundry aired around the world and uncovered Milla's secret compliance. A somber Milla sat on the floor of her closet folding clothes, when the phone rang. Brooke was on the other end and asked if she could stop by. Milla agreed and figured she was in town to discuss their joint venture. Malcolm refused to answer her calls and she could use the company. When Brooke arrived, she entered with a smile and some lunch. The two new friends made small talk while noshing on salmon Caesar salads and fruit cups. After lunch, Brooke began to share her story with Milla. After making a fool out of herself on Football Fiancés and abandoning her eldest child Bradley, Brooke became a mother twice more and ended up homeless. While hiding out at a homeless shelter with her youngest two children her son Bradley's stepmother discovered them and reunited her with her son. She was at the lowest place of her life yet her ex-boyfriend's wife was her saving grace. "Do you know how wretched I felt for my ex's wife to find me that day? Brooke asked Milla. "This woman had raised my son when I abandoned him and still had the love of God in her heart to lift me up," Brooke stated. Milla cried as Brooke shared her story. The only emotion she was capable of feeling was pain and it was the only indication that she was still alive. After explaining how she got back on her feet though having to eat huge slices of humble pie, Brooke encouraged Milla. They both shared the experience of public humiliation and shame. It was Brooke's son's father who filed the lawsuit that ended Football Fiancés. After a time of pouring out before her, Brooke led Milla into a relationship with Jesus Christ. Milla could feel God's love sweep over her. She never knew it was necessary to accept Christ. The room became filled with a strong presence of peace. Somehow unbeknownst to her, Milla knew something inside of her changed. She could feel a breaking within the deepest part of her. After a few hours of fellowshipping with Brooke, Milla realized that Brooke had only come to Vegas to minister to her. That night Brooke boarded a direct flight back to the DMV. Brooke called her daily to pray with her and by the end of the week Milla was feeling brand new. Weeks later during another visit, she and Brooke attended bible study on Tuesday night and worship service on Sunday. Once Milla had a handle on her salvation and the two women agreed upon their business model, Brooke returned to Virginia. The ladies planned to launch in a few months after Milla reluctantly finished season two. She wished she didn't resign her contract and couldn't wait for the season to be over so she could announce her departure. She missed Malcolm desperately but found the strength not to call. Most nights she cried herself to sleep but somehow, she knew everything would be alright. Taping would resume in ten days and she wasn't looking forward to it in the least.

A. Michele Henderson

Sydney rode the elevator to the 19th floor of the media complex. She was called into a private meeting with Kent, Linda and their bosses. After approaching the reception desk, she was escorted to a board room where more than a dozen executives including Kent and Linda were waiting for her. Upon entering she was introduced to the men and women in the room. Eager to know why she was called into the meeting, she quickly sat in her chair to listen. The president of the network told her she was special. He said her popularity ratings among certain demographics had placed her ahead of the other ladies. Sydney loved what she was hearing. She was told that sponsors were ready to give her over a half dozen endorsements which would prove to make her very rich. The team of vultures offered Sydney the opportunity to have her own spinoff if she was willing to "turn up" on season two. They told Sydney if she agreed to some predetermined prerequisites she was as good as gold. The group presented Sydney with a list of things she was required to do so that sponsorship and advertising dollars could be released. Sydney couldn't believe her eyes and ears. When she looked at the list it read:

- Outwardly support the LGBTQ community
- Promote the practice of Yoga and Transcendental Meditation
- Encourage women to freeze their eggs to promote independence from outdated family models
- Promote non-traditional roles for women
- Garner empathy from your assigned demographic by choosing a relatable storyline (fatherlessness, infertility, domestic violence, bullying, an illness or condition, economic disadvantage) and become its poster child

- Allow the cameras to capture the intimate details of your life
- Stage opportunities to promote chosen agendas.

Sydney signed the paper and agreed that her spin off show would include all the requirements for sponsorship. She also agreed to "turn up" for season two and increase viewership. After signing the deal Sydney was offered a new contract for season two. Though she and her cast mates agreed to an additional twelve episodes making $75k each, Sydney was now offered $125k and promised $250k for her spin off. She told Danny about her new deal and they went to Lake Tahoe for a long weekend to celebrate. Sydney wanted to tell him about her children but she couldn't bear for him to leave her now. Taping would begin in seven days and Sydney couldn't wait.

Milla decided to fly to San Diego to spend time with her family. Knowing her humiliation, her father instructed the family not to bring up Malcolm's name. Once back home, Milla visited with family and friends she hadn't seen in years. One evening during dinner, Morgan announced that she was pregnant and everyone rejoiced. Milla noticed the huge rock on Morgan's hand and the convertible Mercedes in her parent's garage. She and Judy were wearing designer clothes from a Parisian designer's current season yet Morgan was a manager at the mall. Morgan's wrist boasted a platinum tennis bracelet and 6 Cartier love bangles. Nobody asked her who the father was and treated it as an informality. Milla was a little sad because she was just beginning to learn about the spiritual implications of fornication and sexual sin. The Abals' weren't a "going to church" kind of family. They believed like many, that they were good people and that was enough to go to heaven. They saw nothing wrong with sexual relationships between two people who loved each other regardless of color, creed or orientation. They had no revelation about God's love for all people being separate from His requirements of righteousness. As the family celebrated the coming of new life, Milla felt led to share about the new life she had found in Christ. Her family listened and smiled. Her mother asked her not to be one of those people who bash others over the head with religion. She explained to her family that Jesus was not about religion but about relationship and how He died and went to hell in our place. She explained His bodily resurrection 3 days and 3 nights later and what that meant for all who'd chose to accept Him as Savior and Lord. Morgan changed the subject with a "good for you MiMi" and began to talk about the baby again. Feeling brushed off for the millionth time, Milla announced that she'd return to Las Vegas the following morning.

While Milla packed her things, Joe asked if they could talk. He shared with Milla how proud he was of her for making the decision to live for God. He told her a story about his great uncle Mack Abal who was a preacher. He said he and uncle Ron would spend summers with Ganny and Grandpy Abal and on Sundays they would attend Grandpy's brother's church. He talked about the bible stories and the love he felt there. He shared his experiences of watching people shout and speak in the Holy Ghost. Milla was shocked! She'd never heard her father talk about God. By the end of summer when he was eight he'd accepted Christ into his heart and was baptized. When he'd return home, his parents thought it was foolishness and during the rest of the year he and uncle Ron adapted.

Summer would return and they'd get fired back up until it was time to go back home. This happened summer after summer until he was twelve. The following year Grandpy died and just a few months later Ganny followed. After that Joe and uncle Ron stayed home during the summers and the practice of spirituality soon faded away. Joe told Milla that the next time she came to visit, they would attend service together. Milla smiled a wide smile and held her father tight.

There was just three days left before taping resumed and the ladies were called into a meeting with the producers. During the meeting, each lady was told what to expound upon in her storyline. Each woman was told how important it was to hold the attention of their viewers. The creative direction of the show called for more intimate details than the previous season. The team wanted Taylor to return to the house where Jason found Jewel eating cat food, the weekend he was scheduled to keep her. They also wanted to go deeper into the depths of her crystal meth addiction and speak to her family and friends. Taylor agreed in front of all the ladies because like Sydney, she had been called into a secret meeting and promised more money and her own show. The team wanted Savannah to stage immigration problems and imply an association with radical practitioners of her faith. Savannah was insulted and appalled. When she refused to portray a derogatory image of her people, the show planned to reduce her screen time in half. Next was Leslie who was asked to visit her mother on camera dressed to the nines and arriving in a Bentley to the projects. Leslie agreed. Lastly, they asked Milla to leave Malcolm on film and begin a new life without him. His team had won the NBA Championship and they knew the drama would create numbers. Milla agreed, because she'd be able to share Christ, with everyone who was watching for a scandal. Sydney sat at the meeting like a fly on turd hill, believing that she would be the biggest reality star of all time.

When Milla arrived at home, she decided she would shut in for a couple of days to mentally prepare for the show. She hadn't seen or heard from Malcolm in months and knew the show was negotiating the terms of their reunion. When she checked her messages, Brooke encouraged her to attend a worship service in the area. When she called Brooke in Virginia to gather the details, she was intrigued. Brooke's son's father was a pastor whose friend was in Las Vegas for a time of revival. His name was Josiah Carter and according to Brooke, he was the real deal. He was also baptizing new believers that night and Milla wanted to get baptized just like Joe. She agreed and told Brooke that she would tell her all about it the next day.

By 7pm Milla entered the Holy Tabernacle of Christ for Thursday night service. She had her Louis Vuitton Keepall full of the essentials she needed for baptism. Before service, Pastor Josiah's wife Joelle shared her testimony. Milla cried as she spoke about surviving an abusive relationship. Malcolm never physically wounded Milla but the verbal and psychological abuse was just as bad. The power of God filled the place and it set the tone for the evening. After a powerful sermon, Pastor Josiah had an altar call for salvation. Though Milla had already accepted Christ, she wanted to do so in public. When she joined the group in asking Christ to live in her heart, she was immediately engulfed by the love of God. All the acceptance she sought her entire life had been given to her in one moment. For the first time, she felt accepted, understood and loved. One of the altar workers placed oil on her forehead and prayed for her before she returned to her seat. Shortly after, the praise team led the congregation in a beautiful worship song while a woman named Luna, received her deliverance. Milla watched as Luna transformed before her eyes. She hadn't ever seen anything like it. After Luna had her moment with God, the pool was opened for baptism. That night, while Milla waited patiently in line, the love of God became more real to her than life itself. She entered the pool and Pastor Josiah baptized her in Jesus' name. She felt brand new and understood the term of being "born again."

It was the twelfth day of taping when the ladies were called into a special meeting. The show had already followed Taylor to Oklahoma where she exploited herself and Jewel for a quick buck and began a battle between she and Jason. The local media attention made it impossible for Jewel to maintain her privacy and she became thrust into the spotlight against her will. Cameras followed the preteen to school bombarding her with questions she couldn't answer and began showing up at her dance lessons. One reporter managed to get inside the school and harass the innocent child in the cafeteria. Jason promised Taylor he would seek litigation against her for interrupting Jewel's life.

Refusing to skip a beat, the cameras also followed Leslie to St. Louis where she pulled up to the public housing development where her mother lived in a Rolls Royce.

A. Michele Henderson

Dressed in Anne Fontaine apparel, Monika Chiang shoes and carrying a crocodile Hermés HAC 50 as a handbag, Leslie entered her mother's humble abode. The cameras filmed as her mother nodded in and out of consciousness from the drugs she had used prior to taping. With no connection between her and her mother a detached Leslie felt no empathy for the woman who birthed her. The scene included interviews with Leslie's estranged siblings who blamed her for their circumstances though they hadn't seen her in decades. Neighbors and "cousins" berated her for her and Lloyd's lush lifestyle and attempted to bury her in shame. Family members asked her for cars, jewelry, clothes and electronics. She denied their requests and found it interesting that nobody asked for tuition or vocational training. Leslie became disgusted with herself when she realized the image her storyline was promoting rather than her original intent for being on the show. She felt a heaviness cloak her and guilt rested in the pit of her stomach. Realizing she had been used to perpetuate a damaging agenda, she asked to stop filming and told the producers she felt sick. The producers agreed and the cameras ended the scene with Leslie handing her mother an envelope full of money before driving away.

Once all the ladies arrived for the special meeting Kent and Linda got down to business. Due to the buzz created by the pending lawsuit against Taylor and the shopping spree Leslie's mother went on and posted to social media, the show was given a once in a lifetime opportunity. The show was granted a two episode, live taping with a seven second delay. Fans would be treated to a special sneak peek before the show's premier. They wanted to cash in on the momentum of the free publicity and there weren't enough episodes finished to premier the show early. The two episode event, would air for two nights for two hours. The advertisers agreed to commercial free airtime with product placement throughout the show. Kent and Linda told the ladies the special airing would be called Casino Wives: The Dinner Party. During the special, unannounced guests would come to the party and they'd be forced to improvise. The women were offered a million dollars each if they were willing to sign. Sydney and Taylor signed immediately. Moments later Leslie agreed to sign while Savannah and Milla signed reluctantly. Linda informed the women that their filming schedule for the series would not be interrupted and the special episode would air in three nights.

When Leslie arrived home that evening Lloyd was watching television. She told him about the new deal and he told her to use it as an opportunity to promote positivity since it wouldn't be subject to editing. He knew how bad she felt about the angle they chose in St. Louis and hoped she'd get to show the world what a great woman she really was. Lloyd knew what is was to be misunderstood and was thankful that fighting in the streets of Chicago turned into a career instead of a cell or a grave.

Savannah prepared dinner for her family and wondered what Kent and Linda were doing. She saw them for the snakes they were and knew they couldn't be trusted. Who were the individuals that would show up to this dinner party? Savannah resolved to keep her poker face on, no matter what!

Sydney couldn't wait to use the live taping as her breakout moment. Kent encouraged her to pull out all the stops. He gave her a blank check to increase viewership at all cost. She would finally get revenge on everyone who said she'd never amount to anything. It was her time to shine and she couldn't wait. Milla went home just as annoyed as she was when she left. The more she learned about the Lord, the more she loathed being on the show. She wanted to use her platform to share Christ and now her opportunity had come. She was going to take a stand and dare to be different. Before bed, she spoke to her father and Brooke and each of them gave her the courage to stand firm.

Taylor sat in the tub in her and Dale's suite doing drugs. The pressure of the spotlight and the pitfalls of infamy were too much to handle. Taylor had been running from her past but the show forced her to relive it and now she needed help to cope.

Kent and Linda went to dinner to celebrate. They had successfully convinced all the ladies to sign for a million dollars each while they were on target to walk away with over nineteen million each. In their years of creating shows they learned that everyone had a price. They had a knack for magnifying the flaws of broken people and connecting with the viewer's need to be better than someone. Someone like Taylor could be scrutinized by everyone from the obese virgin in Oregon to the forty-year-old man still living at home, because they'd never abandon a child. Shows like theirs gave people the opportunity if just for an hour per week to escape their miserable lives and sit on the proverbial high horse. After all, it's acceptable in America for the poor to mock the rich, the ugly to mock the beautiful, the weak to mock the strong and the nameless to mock the famous. The business partners had surprises popping up every fifteen minutes. The first night included Larry and Dr. Bling with preoperative pictures of Sydney. Taylor went to Kent and Linda and spilled Sydney's secrets. The two of them were speechless when they saw the original Sydney and knew it would make great television. They also contacted Larry who sold her out for $10k. Larry would be placed into a scene with Sydney and Danny as Larry confirms the existence of their two children and provides photos of the original Sydney Kane. If Sydney denies the photos are real, Dr. Bling will be waiting with the proof of his work. Sydney's signing of a release form for his photo gallery allows the doctor to show the photos without legal ramifications. The episode would also include Dale coming out the closet to Taylor and Malcolm's admission of another child to Milla. Night two would document the aftermath of the dinner party and the addition of a new character to the show. Kent and Linda knew Sydney would be blindsided but it had to be done.

The production team worked tirelessly with an event coordinator to convert a hotel ball room into a celebration fit for royalty. Custom chairs had been made displaying the suits of a deck of cards. Tufted red velvet walls were adorned with rhinestones. Black leather tables were made for the occasion. Crystal chandeliers hung from the ceilings and fine china was placed on the tables. A platform was created for the jazz band that would play for the evening and for any invited guest who had an announcement. The centerpieces were made of spades, clovers, diamonds and hearts. The ladies would receive an invitation the following day instructing them what color to wear. Savannah, Leslie and Taylor were asked to wear black, Milla was asked to wear white and Sydney was asked to wear red. The largest sponsor for the special was a wine company who created custom bottles for the show to be sold on their website for viewers to buy. Chefs were hired to cook and butlers to serve. The episode was advertised from coast to coast though viewers would watch live, according to Eastern Standard Time. Social media views of the commercials went viral and many celebrities expressed their excitement to watch.

It was the morning of the live taping and Milla woke up feeling troubled. Her stomach was in knots and she couldn't shake it off. She dreaded the idea of the live show and wanted desperately to walk away. She'd already signed the deal, cashed the check and knew she would have legal issues if she pulled a no show. Losing against the uneasiness that cloaked her like blanket, Milla made her way to the bathroom to take a shower. When she opened the vanity draw to retrieve a shower cap, she noticed an anti-anxiety capsule rolling around the draw. Deciding to take the pill to calm her nerves, Milla swallowed it down with water from the sink that she cupped with her hand. While luxuriating in the shower with her kai bath products, she felt the drug begin to work. Knowing it provided a false sense of calm, Milla felt at peace just the same. After drying off she entered her closet for something to wear. Deciding that less was more she grabbed a pair of jeans, a fresh white t-shirt, a white blazer and a pair of Nike Upstep Cinderella sneakers. She plaited her hair into two French braids, spritzed her neck with Gypsy Water and grabbed her Fendi 2Jours handbag. Walking out of her bedroom she put on her Rolex and a makeup free Milla went to meet Savannah for breakfast.

Savannah sensed that Milla was different this season and wanted to get to know her better. During breakfast, Milla shared with Savannah about her encounter with God. Though Savannah was a devout Hindu she respected everyone's choice to become a better person. She didn't know much about Jesus but she knew Milla was special. The new friends bonded over their moral compass and red velvet pancakes. As fashionistas they discussed their yearly wish lists and made plans to shop together. Savannah was casually dressed in jeans, a crisp white blouse, Gucci Princetown loafers and carrying a Gucci Marmont Maxi bag. Milla put Savannah up on the Supreme and Louis Vuitton collaboration and Savannah put Milla up on Jennifer Le footwear. On a serious note the women agreed that Kent and Linda were no good and made a pact not to return to the show after season two.

After breakfast Milla decided to do some shopping. While thinking about her life she decided to focus on the positive. Once season two was over, she planned to invite Brooke and Savannah on a girl's trip to London. Both women had proven themselves to be a great source of strength and Milla was so thankful for their friendship. She needed to get away and desperately wanted relief from the turmoil that bubbled inside of her. Brooke and Savannah were so confident and Milla yearned for their level of esteem. While browsing her favorite boutiques she bought a pair of Fendi Karlito slip-ons and a matching charm for her 2Jours bag. At Louis Vuitton she bought the Graceful MM in Damier Ebene and a bandeau to tie onto the strap. Milla loved beauty products and decided to grab the Urban Decay Naked Heat palette and a fresh bottle of By Killian's, Single Malt. After glancing at her watch, she realized it was time to go home and rest before the live taping. Before going to her car she stopped at Godiva for her favorite ice cream cone and bought a box of chocolate covered strawberries to enjoy later that night.

That evening the women went into hair and makeup to prepare for the live show. Everyone's nerves were through the roof and each woman had plans in her heart about what to do with the money earned from the special. Before they knew it, it was show time and the theme song began to play. As each woman entered the dining room they were surprised that it was a dinner party in full swing. With over a hundred partygoers in the room dancing, drinking and having a good time the ladies were pleasantly surprised. Many of the partygoers were popular people on the Las Vegas social scene as well as hotel and casino employees. As the ladies drank and mingled with the guests, Kent and Linda's plans began to unfold. Dale stood on the stage and asked for everyone's attention. When the room was quiet he removed a velvet box from his jacket and said he had an announcement to make. With everyone watching, Taylor began to cry thinking he was about to propose. Dale announced that he was in love and now was the time to tell the world. He took the microphone down into the crowd, walked passed Taylor and proposed to Evan the club dee-jay. Everyone stood with their mouths open as Dale's proposal was accepted. Evan grabbed the mic and announced that he was the newest member of the cast. A devastated Taylor lunged at Dale and attacked him until security removed her from the party. Savannah new Kent and Linda were messy and retreated to a corner of the room. Milla grew anxious and she fought the urge to leave.

What else did the producers have up their sleeves. Leslie and Sydney were shocked but continued to have a good time. Malcolm entered the room and upon seeing him, Milla ran into the restroom. Once inside Milla began to panic. She wanted to go home and felt an urgency to leave. Milla began to splash her face with water but soon was so on edge that she began to vomit. Once she gathered her composure she sat on the bathroom floor and began to pray. Still she felt an urgency to leave but was afraid to be confronted by Malcolm for the world to see.

The party continued and a familiar voice could be heard over the microphone. Sydney's heart dropped into her shoes when Larry introduced himself. With the spotlight on her, Sydney's body began to betray her and she began to shake uncontrollably. Behind Larry was a projection screen where Jill and Richie's pictures appeared. Larry announced to Danny that the children belonged to him and Sydney. The room rumbled in shock because Sydney claimed to be childless. To add insult to injury the next photo was a picture of the original Sydney Marie Kane. The room stood in awe as the red headed, small lipped, flat chested, pale skinned and snaggle toothed Sydney was revealed. Danny couldn't believe his eyes. Sydney's head began to spin and the room closed in on her. She grabbed four bottles of wine and headed toward Larry. With just a few yards between them she hurled the first bottle at him and it slammed against the adjacent wall and shattered. As the second bottle left her hand, an emotional Milla quickly came around the corner to leave. The force of the bottle cracked Milla in the head causing her to fall backward onto the corner of the stage where she died on impact. Without hesitation, Sydney continued to throw bottles three and four which hit Larry in the arm and shoulder. Without recognition of what she'd done to Milla, Sydney wrapped herself around Danny's leg as he dragged her on the floor behind him. Crying hysterically and yelling "I can explain, don't leave me" Sydney pleaded with Danny. Security pulled her off of his leg and flung her to the floor.

Malcolm ran to Milla's side as blood poured out from her head. The cameras continued to film and though there was a seven second delay the signal hadn't been suspended. 5 million viewers watched as Milla Abal's life came to an end. Malcolm cried as he held her lifeless body in his arms. Savannah rushed to his side and tried to perform CPR. When the paramedics arrived they pronounced her dead at the scene. Finally, the live show was preempted and media outlets began arriving at the hotel. When the police arrived they sealed the room as a crime scene and everyone cried in disbelief.

Joe called Malcolm's phone over and over for an hour. He and the family had been watching until the show went off the air and he needed answers. Joe continued to call as he and Judy drove to the airport. While Joe and Judy sat at the gate awaiting their flight, Malcolm returned their call. Hearing those dreaded words, Joe fell to his knees and dropped the phone. When Judy picked up the phone, Malcolm told her Milla was gone. Judy fell on the airport floor and had a heart attack. When the paramedics arrived, Joe was "no more good". Malcolm told him to make sure Judy was okay and he would fly them private to Las Vegas when she was stable.

Chapter 4: Facing the Facts

*T*HE following morning a national media circus ensued. National television shows, entertainment news and integral media platforms swarmed Las Vegas like anxious bees. The issue of reality television and the images they portray became a hot topic. Many "experts" were interviewed concerning the nation's appetite for gossip, violence, sex and voyeurism. Advocacy groups for everything from women's rights to healthy images for young girls weighed in. A cease and desist order was issued for all media platforms where the viral video of Milla's death was played.

Sydney

Being arrested for Milla's murder was a shock to Sydney. She sat in a holding cell thinking about how to make things right with Danny. She knew Milla didn't deserve to be killed but she stepped into the altercation Sydney was having with Larry. Surely this would all be sorted out when the cameras documented what really happened, she thought. Hours went by and Sydney hardly noticed, because she was focused on Danny and how to get him back. Later that evening a finely dressed man in a pinstripe suit appeared in front of her. Oblivious to how much trouble she was in, Sydney was brought back to reality when Jonah Sparks esquire, introduced himself. He informed Sydney that he'd been retained by Shelby to defend her. For what? Sydney asked. Jonah responded with a disgusted look on his face "murder," said Jonah. Sydney heard his words and realized that her actions were being taken out of context. "I wasn't trying to hurt her, I was mad at Larry," Sydney stated. "It was an accident, everyone knows that" Sydney said matter-of-factly. "That may be true Ms. Kane but your colleague lost her life" said Jonah. "I will tell the judge myself since you don't understand what happened" said Sydney. "Ms. Kane, the entire country has seen the footage of you murdering Milla Abal, I'm not here to get you acquitted, I've been hired by your mother to make sure you don't receive the death penalty for it" said Jonah. "You're fired" said Sydney, "I don't want a lawyer who thinks I'm guilty". "No problem Ms. Kane, I will let your mother know" Jonah said as the officer led him out of the holding area.

The next morning an officer called Sydney's name and she jumped up in excitement thinking she was being released. When he cuffed and shackled her, she resisted. "What are you doing? I just made bail" said Sydney. "No ma'am you're going before the judge for arraignment," the officer stated. "Great said Sydney, I will tell him I'm not guilty." When Sydney walked out of the police station she was met by protesters yelling obscenities and chanting "murderer." Many protesters were wearing Kane killed Abal T-shirts. Reporters swarmed the police van flashing cameras and asking how she felt. Sydney was naïve enough to believe that it was all just a misunderstanding.

During arraignment judge Michael A. Wilkins read the charges against Sydney including murder in the 2nd degree. He asked for her plea to which she said not guilty in a mocking fashion. Judge Michael told Sydney it was unwise not to have an attorney and to make light of the charges she was facing. Since there was more than enough proof against Sydney, he ordered her to remain in custody until trial. Sydney had no clue what was in store for her but she was transferred to the Florence McClure Women's Correctional Center.

That evening while Sydney submitted to the intake process of prison she finally realized it wasn't a game. Inmates yelled at her as she walked through general population with the guards which caused her to hang her head. Panic began to set in and her body betrayed her. Down Sydney's leg and onto the floor was a trail of loose stool. Knowing what had just happened in front of all those people Sydney's body betrayed her once more and she had a nervous breakdown. The women erupted into laughter mocking her as she was taken to the medical ward. A custodian arrived with a mop to clean up the feces and the women laughed hysterically. For the next eleven months awaiting trial Sydney was no longer called by her name but by a name beginning with an S and ending with a Y with the same number of syllables.

Thousands of people filed into the Las Vegas Convention Center to pay their respects to Milla. Fans and Johnny-come-latelys alike, held up signs and wore t-shirts with Milla's image on them. Many people recounted stories about how special she was including Savannah. After her flowers were given, she was eulogized by Pastor Josiah

Carter. He had only met Milla on the evening she was baptized but could stand in full assurance that Milla was now with God. He made certain to tell the congregants present and those watching around the world that God had nothing to do with Milla's untimely death. He explained to the secular audience that Milla's death was the result of a human being exercising her free will and actions. Josiah taught the listeners that God has given mankind dominion over the earth and therefore only through a relationship with Him will he impose His will on us. "You have the right to accept or reject Him because God seeks relationships not prisoners," taught Josiah. "You cannot serve Satan and look to God to make it alright, no more than you can work at Target and get your insurance from Best Buy" said Josiah. He cautioned those in attendance that just like Milla, nobody knew the day or hour of their death. He then added that like Milla they could choose life. After a rousing 33 minute sermon, hundreds of funeral goers made their way to the platform to accept Christ as their Savior, including Joe Abal. Altar workers prayed with each one of them and presented the born-again believers with bibles and a 50 state list of churches and ministries. Brooke sat on the platform with pastor Josiah's wife Joelle and couldn't believe Milla was gone. She was so grateful their paths had crossed and would cherish the time they shared together.

Leslie and Lloyd watched the service online from an over water bungalow in Jamaica. She couldn't believe that Sydney had taken Milla's life. She knew about Sydney's children and her plastic surgery but found it cruel that Kent and Linda exploited her pain for shock value and ratings. She knew Sydney was wrong for her actions but hoped Kent and Linda would have their moment of reckoning as well.

That night continued to play over in Leslie's mind. She had no idea why Malcolm had come and found it suspicious. The show was cancelled and Kent, Linda and their entire team were being "investigated." Leslie knew it meant nothing but the outrage heard across the world had to result in filings against the show.

Taylor sat in the bath tub binging cocaine and watching the service on television. Selling Sydney's secrets set off the domino effect to Milla's murder and the guilt was too heavy to carry. She flew to Miami to get away from the circus and had been locked in her condo for eleven days. Linda and Kent paid Taylor $30,000 for dirt on Sydney and half of it was already up her nose. Spiraling out of control and entertaining demonic company, Taylor yielded to her tormentors. It would be another 17 days before the neighbors would complain about a stench, leading to the discovery of Taylor's lifeless body.

Savannah's heart ached as she laid on her bed for a nap. The events of the last two weeks were exhausting. She missed Milla and was thankful for the opportunity to know her. The stress of multiple investigations had taken a toll on her peace and her, Mithush and the children were leaving in the morning to fly to London. There they would stay and reclaim their wholeness, indefinitely. Las Vegas had proven to live up to its name, costing people more than they wanted to pay and taking them further than they wanted to go, sin.

Shelby cried from home watching Milla's service. Everyone was mourning her death but Shelby had lost a daughter too. Long before the glitz and the glam of reality television, Shelby had ceased being a mother and became

Sydney's friend. Shelby knew that Sydney was ill prepared for the real world. She had no formal education and had no idea what it looked like to be a responsible adult. Shelby had failed her daughter and accepted the responsibility of not properly raising her. She wanted her grandchildren's lives to be different and they were her second chance. The shame of walking around Tulsa as folks whispered and stared was too much. Jill and Richie had to be homeschooled because they were constantly harassed for their mother's mistakes. Shelby planned to move her and the children to Utah where they could begin a new life. Larry refused to return her calls so she had him served. Shelby wanted to have legal permanent custody of the children. Without a fight, Larry went to a local attorney and had papers drawn up relinquishing his parental rights to Shelby. After a formal hearing, Shelby was granted sole custody of the children.

Malcolm and Morgan kissed as they laid in bed. Malcolm never had the chance to approach Milla during the live taping so their secret was still safe. The two lovers decided to terminate Morgan's pregnancy until the trial was over. Morgan was secretly relieved that she never had to square off with Milla. She had been having sex with Malcolm since she was 16 years old and now he was all hers. She was tired of watching the man she loved pretend to love her sister every Thanksgiving, Christmas, Easter, Mother's Day and Fourth of July. Morgan and Malcolm reminisced about the times they would have sex once Milla fell asleep. One evening about Five years ago, they were having sex in the laundry room and Judy walked in on them. Without a word, Judy walked away and the three of them made no mention of it. Malcolm and Morgan decided they would act like Milla's death had brought them together and after the trial they would come out as a couple.

Judy sobbed quietly in the shower as the water flooded across her face. Still very sore and weak since her heart attack she couldn't believe her daughter was gone. She and Joe decided to stay in Milla's apartment to personally pack up her things. Her body was being sent to San Diego in the morning and her sister Gloria would take care of Milla's burial arrangements. Judy felt empty inside and couldn't come to terms with all that had happened. Morgan told her a few days before that she had a miscarriage but she knew Morgan all too well. She'd been playing the dumb mother card for years and knew full well what was going on between Malcolm and Morgan behind Milla's back. Judy hoped that they would stop for Milla's sake but it never happened. She turned her head every time Morgan showed up with expensive clothes, diamonds, designer handbags and just recently a new car. Judy knew she didn't give her children religion but she assumed that they'd develop a moral compass of their own. There was a decency that she expected to be present in all human beings. Isn't morality the thing that separates humans from animals, she thought. She was ashamed of Morgan's behavior but loved her just the same. She already had her hands filled with Joe deciding to be a Christian. Judy was one of the rare African American baby boomers who didn't grow up in church. It wasn't a priority in her family and religious people were considered strange. Her father believed that everyone was responsible for their own life and that there was no man in the sky determining who you'd become. Judy stepped out of the shower and prepared for bed. Tomorrow they were going to the hotel to close Milla's boutique.

Brooke was walking through the casino on her way to grab something to eat, when she saw a group of people in Milla's store. She knocked on the door and Joe recognized her from the funeral. She introduced herself and asked if she could help. The family agreed and welcomed her inside. Judy asked Brooke about her relationship with Milla. Brooke shared some of their memories and informed the Abals' that they were about to launch a joint venture. Joe's niece Daphne agreed that Milla was excited and told her about it. Brooke was excited to finally meet Daphne because Milla said she was her favorite cousin. Daphne smiled. "Did she talk about me"? Morgan asked. Brooke looked at Morgan and wished she could give her a piece of her mind but the Holy Ghost tugged on her conscience. "She was excited to meet your baby" Brooke said since it was all she could get away with. Milla confided in Brooke that she believed Morgan was cheating with Malcolm after her visit to san Diego. Morgan hung her head low before needing to "get some air." Brooke knew her shot had met its target and prayed that Morgan would come to terms with her actions. An awkward silence filled the boutique but everyone kept packing boxes. An hour had gone by and Morgan didn't return yet nobody was concerned. Brooke thought it was odd. As her stomach began to growl she remembered she was hungry. With only one rack of clothes left, Brooke excused herself after giving the Abals' her contact information and following Daphne on social media. Joe hugged Brooke tight and thanked her for leading Milla to the Lord. He joked that Judy should be thankful that he wasn't 20 years younger. Judy told Joe he couldn't keep up with her 20 years ago, so Brooke was safe. They all laughed. As Brooke left the boutique, she could see Malcolm and Morgan on a bench far down the hall. "Pull the covers off, Lord" prayed Brooke before walking into the bistro a few doors down.

It was a frigid November morning when Sydney was transferred to Baltimore. She had just become acclimated to her surrounding yet she was forced to adapt again. Each day Sydney spent in prison a piece of her died. The women in Indiana weren't so bad. She had a few scuffles but nothing that landed her in solitary confinement. She'd miss Coleen and Farrah and wished she had the opportunity to say goodbye. Her transfer was taking place a month earlier than expected. Coleen and Farrah were also convicted of murder. Coleen for killing her husband and his mistress and Farrah for killing her daughter's molester. Though their crimes were considered honorable, the two women accepted Sydney with open arms. They worked together in the laundry room and for a short time each week Sydney managed to laugh. Spending her last birthday in prison was a far cry from partying with Leslie and Nino. Farrah and Coleen were much older and encouraged Sydney to look forward to her freedom. They pointed out that at only 27 she would only be 52 when she was released. To Sydney it was an entire lifetime away and she wasn't sure if she had what it takes. During her transfer, she was taken to a prison in Ohio for a few days. Sydney was alone in her cell and didn't talk to anyone. On a blistering Wednesday afternoon, Sydney arrived at Supermax. The correction officers were more stern than her previous guards and she was treated like she wasn't famous. After the intake process, she was given a yellow jumpsuit. She had her choice of footwear between some clunky white shoes or blue slip-ons. She chose the blue slip-ons and later found out they were called Jackie Chans after the martial arts actor. The white shoes she rejected were called Sheila Dixon after the former mayor of Baltimore City. She understood the connection between the slip-ons and martial arts but the Sheila Dixon reference went over her head. Upon entering her cell, she could tell that her roommate didn't want her there. Sydney wasn't use to being around so many black people. She was convinced there were more blacks in this prison than the entire state of Oklahoma. Knowing Leslie didn't prepare her for what she encountered. Leslie was different like Oprah and Steve Harvey. That night Sydney managed to fall asleep. The next morning Sydney made her way to Keefe where she bought snacks for her room. During breakfast, she met some of the women on her tier including her cell mate Trixi. While eating her cereal, she was approached by Tammy who was a fan of the show. Once Tammy began asking questions, a group of women gathered around to hear the answers. Tammy asked about each of the ladies on the show and their storylines. Most of them loved Leslie and Sydney was happy to be able to answer their questions in detail. They had crushes on Lloyd and admired his flashy ways. Sydney told them about Lloyd's closet, plane and cars. The ladies sat in awe as Sydney told them about the opulence and luxuries she experienced because of Leslie. Even though most of the women came from impoverished backgrounds they loved to see people like Lloyd make it out of the hood. Sydney recognized the sense of pride they all shared for seeing someone "make it." The women were sad about Milla and understood how fast life can take a turn for the worse. Sydney told them that Milla was close with Savannah and often read her bible and watched Joyce Meyer sermons. Sydney was surprised that the ladies loved Joyce Meyer and Joel Osteen. Trixi explained to Sydney that growing up in church was often part of the black experience. The women shared stories about their church experiences. Unfortunately, church wasn't a safe-haven for many of them. Quite a few were mishandled and abused by church leaders. Pebbles shared a story about being violated every week by a certain deacon. They all agreed that their parents had blind trust. Sydney was intrigued. Khadijah X mocked the church and offered that blacks shouldn't be Christian anyway and should submit to the teachings of the honorable Elijah Muhammed. The crowd ensued in a heated debate about whether Jesus was black or not and Sydney went back to her cell.

Sydney began working in the Laundry room to stay busy. She had plenty of cash on her books so the $85 she earned each week was a drop in the bucket. She quickly made "friends" by giving away snacks and makeup. Khadijah's roommate Brenda began to cornrow Sydney's hair in exchange for food and Khadijah gave her a hard time. "It wasn't enough to buy our lips and our backside but now you want our hairstyles too, what's left?" Khadijah mocked. Sydney liked Khadijah. Though she riled the other ladies into a frenzy, Sydney enjoyed the free history lessons.

Christmas was just around the corner and Sydney became extremely sad. Her children were writing to her but it only reminded her of her failures. The other women had visitors but nobody had come to see her. The following

Sunday she went to church services but felt more alone than ever. When the opportunity came for her to earn her G.E.D., Sydney jumped at the chance. During the holidays, she stayed in her cell and only came out to work. The prison allowed the women to have parties, but quite a few of them weren't in the holiday spirit. Winter gave way to spring, summer and autumn. Sydney was just weeks away from making it an entire year in Baltimore. She wasn't the same person. She learned that prison was about stuffing your emotions into your socks and existing long enough to make it out. In just one year so many women had come and gone. She'd gone from drinking cocktails with diamonds in her glass to drinking Capri Sun foil packs. From eating truffle fries dipped in caviar to "the hook up." Her palate surely had taken a 180° turn. The hook up as made by her former roommate Trixi, is rice or ramen noodles, broken potato chips, canned sausage, broken pieces of honey bun and queso mixed together. Others use canned herring or sardines.

One afternoon during lunch, the entire facility was locked down. A fight broke out among six inmates leading to one woman being unconscious. The following day Sydney learned it was a lover's quarrel amid allegations of cheating. Sydney may've been lonely but 25 years wasn't long enough for her to be attracted to women. She knew about the P.R.E.A. act and was thankful for its existence. Not many inmates were willing to force themselves on someone in exchange for more time.

Sydney was excited when her G.E.D. came in the mail. She couldn't wait to tell Shelby on their bi-weekly call. When she dialed Shelby's house she barely recognized her voice. She gave Shelby the news about her diploma and Shelby told her she was proud. As usual the children didn't want to speak to her which Sydney learned to stuff down. Shelby told Sydney she'd been diagnosed with ovarian cancer and had been doing Chemotherapy for a few weeks. Sydney began to cry and slid down the wall. When she hung up the phone she called her lawyer. She told him about her mother and asked if that would be cause for her release if something happened to Shelby. Sydney was amazed that her children's possible misplacement had no bearing on her conviction. Sydney went back to her cell to cry. The following day the women asked her what was going on and she told them. They were shocked that Sydney had no clue about the ramifications of being a convicted felon. Five of the seven women she was talking to entered prison without knowing what would become of their children. A couple women had a friend or family member step up but the other women's children were in the system. As more women joined the conversation Sydney learned that over a dozen women on her tier, have children under state guardianship. Some women were even aware that their children had been abused. Almost all the women had a relative pass during their stay but only a few were able to attend their parent's funeral. "I guess you're earning that backside after all" mocked Khadijah. "By year 25 you just might understand what it means to be black" she laughed. The women gave each other high fives and pounds. Hopelessness fell on Sydney and despair over came her.

A few days later Sydney attempted suicide in the laundry room when she drank some bleach. Collapsing to the floor she began to vomit and became violently ill. During the 10 minutes it took for the ambulance to arrive,

Sydney went into cardiac arrest. She was rushed to shock trauma where the attending physicians fought to save her life. For the following three days Sydney was placed in intensive care. Shelby flew to Maryland and was given special permission to be by her daughter's bedside. The children were sent to Oklahoma City where Larry's great aunt looked after them. When Sydney regained consciousness she was so happy to see her mother. "I'm sorry" was all she could muster the words to say. Shelby held her emaciated child in her arms. Sydney's pain was unbearable, why didn't she die. Shelby was at least sixty pounds lighter than when she last saw her. The guilt of never going back home and checking on her family was all too much to bear. Her children hated her, her life was ruined and she was a convicted murderer. What hope could she have for a better life. Shelby apologized to Sydney for not being a better mother. She confessed that she should've done better. The two women held each other for what seemed like a lifetime. Shelby shared with Sydney that she had found God through her treatment process. She and the children had been going to church and Shelby felt more hopeful. Sydney wished she had hope but emptiness was the only feeling she possessed. That evening when Shelby left the hospital she knew she wouldn't see Sydney again. After two weeks at the University of Maryland Medical Center, Sydney was sent to a maximum security psychiatric hospital.

Joe stood in the sanctuary at Living Water Church with his hands lifted in worship. He and Judy's divorce was final and he wasn't looking back. Their marriage had been irreparable when Judy confessed to covering up Morgan's relationship with Malcolm. Those two heathens stood in a courtroom talking about Milla's character when they had none to speak of. How dare Malcolm look him in his face and ask for Milla's hand in marriage while thumping around with Morgan. She sat across from her sister and announced that baby as if she'd won the lottery. He was even more appalled that Malcolm was choosing to tell Milla about him and Morgan's relationship and embarrass her on national television. Those vultures wouldn't go unpunished but Joe was earnestly trying to hand them over to God. After service one of the congregants congratulated him on Morgan and Malcolm's wedding. The world was under the impression that the two of them found each other amidst tragedy. Joe declined the sentiment and told brother Bill that he didn't approve of the wedding or the relationship. Brother Bill apologized before walking away. On his way home, Joe stopped at the store to buy a new DVD release. While in the electronics department of the store, Sydney's suicide attempt was on the national news. Joe had no idea she was in Baltimore, they were told she'd be in Indiana. Many of the customers gathered around the television to listen. Joe decided to quickly pay for his purchase and drive home. That night Joe couldn't sleep so he went to his prayer closet to pray. That night he communed with God in a way he never thought possible. Joe not only was given an unusual assignment, he was also given the strength to perform it.

Sydney spent most of her days in a trance. The medications she was given had left her as a shell of her former self. One afternoon she was sitting in the cafeteria of the hospital when she glanced at a book the woman next to her was reading. She asked the woman if she could look at the back cover and the woman obliged. The author of the book was the same woman she'd met in the spa before the premier of Casino Wives. "I've met her, you know" Sydney said proudly "I've met the tooth fairy, so now we're even" mocked the woman. "What's the book about," inquired Sydney. "It's about a woman's journey to find God" said the woman in a taunting fashion. "Because of her books, I'm able to see my situation in a different way. She uses situations people can relate to and shows them another view," the woman said proudly. "Can I read one" Sydney asked? "No I can't loan you one" said the woman. Within a week, Sydney had convinced the woman to loan her a book. By the following week she had read all three books of the trilogy. There was a character named Apple in three of them who Sydney could relate to. All they both ever wanted was to be loved. If Apple's life could recover after a mistake leading to death, maybe Sydney's could too.

Shelby flew into Oklahoma City to pick up the children before returning to Utah. While waiting for her bags Shelby felt weak and asked the lady beside her to dial 911. Shelby collapsed on the floor at the baggage claim area and was rushed to Integris Baptist Medical Center. Shelby always carried her medical records with her and handed them over to the paramedics. The stress of her trip to Baltimore coupled with her weakened condition was too much for Shelby's body. The following morning Shelby was eating breakfast when a familiar face walked in. Tears flooded Shelby's eyes when she saw Jillian. Shelby was overcome with emotion and couldn't compose herself. "Hi Momma Shell" said Jillian in the sweetest voice. The two women just held each other and cried. Jillian knew all about Sydney's woes. She hadn't ever watch Casino Wives but Sydney's infamy crossed over into mainstream media. Just days ago,

Jillian watched in horror as the news reported Sydney's suicide attempt. After about an hour Shelby learned that Jillian was now married with two natural children and one adopted child. Her husband Keith was an electrician and Baptist minister. Shelby was so proud of Jillian for turning her life around. Shelby told Jillian about the children and her failing health. Jillian always loved Shelby and was moved with compassion. For the next few days Shelby remained at Integris. The doctors consulted with her doctors back in Utah and Shelby's treatments would become more aggressive when she arrived home. Shelby was hoping to see Jillian before she was discharged because she had been off the previous couple days. Not long after, Jillian walked in with a handsome man resembling actor Dean Cain. Jillian introduced her husband Keith Grant to Shelby. She also went on to tell Shelby that the Lord told her to look after Jill and Richie. Shelby was so grateful. She'd been praying for months for God to send someone she could entrust the children to because Larry was an alcoholic and his family declined. His great aunt who had been watching the children for over a week was 73 years old and couldn't keep them long term. For the next few days Shelby stayed in Oklahoma preparing the children for yet another transition. Thankfully the children were excited to stay with Keith and Jillian. Jill knew she was named after her and Richie was too young to understand. Shelby decided to stay in Oklahoma City and receive her treatments there. After a brief trip to Utah to gather the essentials, Shelby settled in a small apartment and began more aggressive treatments. Over the following month, Shelby, Jillian and Keith hired a lawyer to transfer custody of the children and begin the adoption process. Once legal custody was given to the Grants, Shelby gave them $2 million dollars for the children's care. Shelby told Keith and Jillian to spend it however they saw fit. After a lengthy battle and outliving the doctor's predictions three times, Shelby Kane went home to be with the Lord.

Sydney was sitting in an afternoon bible study when the nurse and doctor walked in. They told Sydney that her mom had passed away but not to worry about her children because Jillian was going to raise them. Sydney was completely shocked. How did her mom find Jill after all these years? The doctor told Sydney that she was unable to be released for the funeral considering her condition. The nurse stood beside him prepared to medicate her but Sydney didn't put up a fight. The following morning Sydney phoned her attorney and asked if she could be transferred back to prison. Just a week later, Sydney was back at Chesapeake. She was excited to see Khadijah and Tammy. Over the next few weeks Sydney found hope in small things. She wasn't allowed to return to the laundry room so she worked in the kitchen as a dishwasher. One afternoon while lying in her bunk watching television, she received an unlikely letter. She couldn't believe her eyes as she read it. Tears began falling down her face and onto the page. The love of God encompassed her in such a tangible way. Hope began to flood her heart and mind and at that very moment, she knew God was real.

Dear Sydney,

I pray this letter finds you in health and strength. The amazing thing about God is that you cannot truly love Him without loving others. Almost four years ago, my life came to a screeching halt when I witnessed the death of my eldest daughter on national television. Just days prior, she and I sat in her childhood bedroom talking about the plan and promise of God. She had just come into the knowledge of her Savior and the author of her life. I'd never seen her eyes so bright and her heart so pure. My Milla had finally found her place. For years, I watched helplessly as my biracial daughter struggled in a world where she never fit in. Rejected by both sides of her ethnicity for nothing more than being born, there was nothing my "white privilege" could do to help. She struggled through her formative years and dealt with stints of depression and anxiety. When she ran off to Las Vegas for love I thought surely, she'll be happy now. I was wrong. The public scrutiny of dating a professional athlete proved to be a toxic combination for a young woman who struggled with her self-esteem. Then she opened the boutique. Ever since she was a child Milla loved fashion. Surely, she'd be happy now! Instead, Malcolm's groupies would come to the boutique to steal, mock her for his cheating ways and harass her. Then she joined the cast of Casino Wives and my precious baby girl was thrown to the wolves. As you're learning the hard way, fame only magnifies what's already there. All your insecurities, character flaws and struggles are placed on front street for public consumption. Why am I telling you all this, you might ask? Because the last time I saw my daughter she'd found her place of peace. I can rest at night knowing that she's in the loving presence of God. Sydney, I know about your suicide attempt, the small children you left behind and the actions you took, to fill the gaping hole in your soul. I watched every episode of Casino Wives and I saw a scared little girl wanting so desperately to be loved and accepted. I offer you what Milla found. I'm offering you an opportunity to collect the broken pieces of your life and become a better person. Sydney Marie Kane, I FORGIVE YOU!!!! May you seek rest in Christ for your weary soul and forgiveness of your sins.

Sincerely,

Joseph Richard Abal

Ps: If you're serious about following Christ, feel free to write me from time to time.

Chapter 5: The Harvest

MORGAN sat in the master suite of her and Malcolm's mansion fanning herself. She hadn't felt well for the past few weeks and felt in her heart that she was pregnant. Excitedly she walked into the bathroom to take a home pregnancy test. She wasn't sick at all during the pregnancy she and Malcolm decided to terminate but knew every pregnancy was different. After a few minutes her results were negative so she took a second test. The results were negative as well, so she decided to make an appointment the following day with her doctor. Malcolm had the flu a few weeks prior and she may've caught it from him. After scheduling her appointment, she walked into her closet to lay out her clothes for the following day. When she opened the drawer to her closet island she saw the program from Milla's funeral. An eerie feeling surrounded Morgan at the sight of her sister's face. Guilt rose within her and nausea gripped her body. Before she could make it to the bathroom, Morgan began to vomit violently. Her body became weak and she broke out in a cold sweat. Morgan began to shiver before fainting on the floor.

Hours later Morgan came to herself and sat upright on her bedroom floor. She was home alone so there was nobody there to help her. She got up and walked into the bathroom to shower and shampoo her hair. Once dry and dressed for bed she dialed Malcolm but the call went straight to voicemail. The Dice weren't playing for the next two nights so she wondered where he was. She began to cry knowing he was probably with another woman. For years, she had to remain his secret while he and Milla were together but now she had to share him with groupies from all over the world. She decided to call her mother to vent but Judy didn't answer the phone either. Since her parent's divorce, Judy had been doing the most. She had gone to Dr. Bling for a body makeover after seeing the miracles he performed with a cannula. Judy had breast augmentation, liposuction, rhinoplasty and a Brazilian butt lift. She has gone from a size 12 to a size 4 and had utterly lost her mind. She was outwardly dating guys young enough to be her sons and was officially a mom gone wild. Outside of Judy, Morgan didn't have anyone. She didn't talk to her father often because he was always "judging" her and her cousins and "friends" stopped talking to her once she married Malcolm. How could it be wrong to marry the man she loved? Malcom was her first and only, yet people treated her as if she was promiscuous. Morgan rode down to the kitchen in the elevator to prepare something to eat. While downstairs she turned on the 6pm news as she prepared to make dinner. Morgan decided to whip up a pan of lobster alfredo. She already had cooked lobster tails in the fridge and placed a Sur-la-table pot and pan on the stove. She filled the pot with salted water to cook the cavatappi, and added heavy cream, garlic and cracked pepper into the pan with melted butter and olive oil. Morgan decided to add a handful of spinach, sundried tomatoes and the lobster before finishing the sauce off with fresh grated parmesan cheese. She'd have plenty of leftovers the following day and sat at the island to enjoy her meal. Morgan poured herself a glass of white wine and broke off a piece of bread from a baguette on the counter. The news anchors joked about a local animal who escaped from the zoo before a breaking news story preempted the segment. A burning aircraft could be seen with black billowing smoke. As Morgan ate her meal, she almost choked when the pictures of Kent and Linda were plastered on the news. The two of them were killed in a private jet crash while leaving Cancun, Mexico. The story included a montage of their reality shows and pictures of Sydney and Milla. They played a video of Milla's memorial service and showed pictures of Milla and Malcolm. Nausea gripped Morgan's body as she began to sweat and she vomited on the kitchen floor.

Judy Abal relished in the pleasure of her company. She hadn't felt this young in years. Thankful to be free of her marital constraints, she lived for her weekly romp. After years of quickies in the garage and pantry, she and Malcolm could take their time. He's been a good lover over the years and she taught him well. Since she caught him with Morgan, Judy too has been enjoying Malcolm's prowess. For years, he's been the silver lining in her marriage to Joe. Judy had been dying to be free from the boredom that became her life. She felt terrible about losing her daughter and the destruction of her family. For years, she stayed in a lifeless marriage and did the best she could. Nobody taught her about life, her parents were too busy trying to keep food on the table. Now was the time for Judy to live for herself. She knew what it was and didn't get things twisted.

Unlike her daughters, she wasn't in love and used the young athlete for intimacy and modern comforts. The young girls of this generation were too busy wanting to be seen but Judy was old school. She wanted A+ credit and $0 balances. Judy's new condo was paid in full with the deed in her name, she had the title to her new Audi truck, close to a million in cash and her 401k from working for 30 years as a federal employee. You could call Judy Abal many things but you couldn't call her naive.

The following morning Morgan arrived at her doctor's appointment. She tested for pregnancy before she left home and still the results were negative. She didn't sleep well thinking about her sister and was glad to get out of the house. During her appointment, her doctor prescribed her a Z-Pak for her symptoms and sent her to the lab for bloodwork since she thought she was newly pregnant. He told Morgan he'd call her with the results. She left the office and decided to look at baby furniture in a local boutique. It was finally going to happen, she and Malcolm were having a baby.

Sydney cried on the phone while catching up with Jillian. It had been years since she heard her voice. Her heart was broken that she couldn't attend her own mother's funeral but was so grateful that Jill had her children. Jillian offered to pray with Sydney to receive Christ but she declined. Though Shelby, Joe and Jillian all believed, Sydney wasn't sure. She was excited that her children spoke of God and hoped she'd one day see what everyone else saw. For the first time in the four years she'd been at Chesapeake, Sydney placed pictures on her wall. Jill had sent her pictures of the children and pictures they'd taken with Shelby before she passed. While Sydney thought about Jill and how she wished she'd returned to school with her, Khadijah and Trixi came to her cell. Surprised that she finally put pictures on the wall, her 2 tier mates, looked on in admiration. Almost forgetting why they came, Trixi handed Sydney the newspaper with Kent and Linda's deaths on the front page. Sydney covered her mouth as she read the article. When she looked up at the ladies they were smiling and nodding. They joined together in an embrace and Sydney cried on their shoulders. For years Kent and Linda took no responsibility for the circumstances they created. They weren't celebrating their deaths but they stood in a silent agreement that Kent and Linda's deeds had come full circle.

Forty five miles away, Brooke stood in her boutique reading the Washington Post and eating a piece of butter cake from Mastro's. She too silently reconciled Linda and Kent's deeds. She had made a fool of herself on Football Fiancés for all the world to see. She also had to live with the awareness that those images she portrayed on the show, were the last images her grandmother Mae saw of her before she died. The news of the plane crash spread throughout their community. A news story pointed out how nobody on any of the shows sent condolences to the families. Britney Joseph posted: "On behalf of myself and the sisterhood of Football Fiancés, Glam Wives and Casino Wives we send our heartfelt condolences to the families of Linda and Kent" followed by praying hand emojis. All the ladies who were able, liked the post in solidarity.

Morgan was in the dressing room of a high- end department store, when the phone rang. It was her doctor calling about the results of her pregnancy test. "Mrs. Ross, I've received the results of your lab work and I'll need you to come in and see me. You've tested negative for pregnancy and positive for HIV" said Dr. Wong. Morgan slid down the wall of the dressing room in utter disbelief. She ended the call without responding to her physician. Morgan's entire body went numb and she broke out in a cold sweat. As she rehearsed Dr. Wong's words, she rocked back and forth in a trance. Two hours later, she exited the dressing room and made her way to the car. Once she closed the door, silence engulfed her. She sat motionless and expressionless in the car until the mall officer knocked on her window. "Ma'am are you alright? You've been sitting here for hours" he asked. Without acknowledging him, Morgan turned the ignition and began to drive. Once she got home she sat on the couch in a daze. Still awake and sitting on the couch when Malcolm walked in eleven hours later, Morgan sat rocking. Malcolm dropped his bag and approached Morgan with a smile on his face. Noticing her expression, he asked what was wrong. "You gave me HIV" Morgan blurted out. "I gave you what? You ungrateful witch" Malcolm said. "You heard me" said Morgan. "Chick please, ain't nothing wrong with *me* your trifling behind been sleeping around" Malcolm announced. "You're the only person I've ever been with Malcolm, you did this to me" Morgan screamed. "All you women say that but I see what you been doing" Malcolm mocked. "You're nothing like Milla, she was a good girl and you're just loose" Malcolm chided. Morgan snapped and lunged at him scratching and clawing at his face. As he tried to push her off of him, Morgan began to bite him. Gnawing at his face, she broke skin and he began to bleed. Once he freed himself he felt flesh hanging from his face as blood dripped on the marble floor. "You crazy witch, get out of my house before I beat the breaks off you" Malcolm yelled. Morgan ran upstairs and locked herself in their bedroom. Malcolm followed her and kicked the door off the hinges. While hiding in her closet she dialed 911. When the operator answered Morgan said who she was and where she lived and that her husband Malcolm Ross of the Las Vegas Dice was trying to kill her. Once he entered her closet she left the phone line open and laid it where it couldn't be seen. 911 recorded Malcolm beating Morgan while yelling expletives and threatening her life. When the police arrived, he was arrested and Morgan was rushed to the hospital. Her injuries were serious including a broken jaw. The following morning it was all over the news.

Joe was sitting in his breakfast nook listening to the traffic report when he heard the story. Immediately he grabbed his keys and headed to the airport. By early afternoon he was in Las Vegas headed to an area hospital. He cried as he rode in the taxi because it was the first time he'd been back to Vegas since losing Milla. He felt convicted about his laid-back approach to parenting and repented for allowing one individual to ruin both his daughter's lives. Once he arrived at the hospital, Judy was already there. Joe was shocked by her transformation. She'd never looked better. The former spouses embraced and held hands. It was at that moment that Judy realized she missed her husband terribly. Her new life wasn't fulfilling and Joseph Abal was looking mighty fine. He cried as he looked upon his daughter's injuries. "He has to be stopped" Joe said to Judy. With guilt rising in her belly all Judy could do was shake her head in agreement. By that evening, Judy and Joe were devastated with the news of Morgan's diagnosis. Judy began to have chest pains and had to be admitted. Joe thought her heart was too weak to handle the news, he was unaware of Judy's secret. While Joe was with Morgan she asked her doctor to give her the test as well. A day later, Judy's results were negative. She always used protection with Malcolm and never got "caught up." Thankful for the good news she decided to confess to Joe. It was better to tell him the truth all at once than to ration it out over time. Joe was completely floored. He apologized for not being more assertive and for not being the husband she needed. Judy was shocked. Together the two parents stayed by their child's side until she was released. Upon discharge Morgan filed for divorce and moved back to California to live with Judy. Within a week, Malcolm lost all his endorsements and was fired from the team. He was charged with felony domestic battery but was released on bail until trial.

It was a rainy day in London when Savannah arrived on Brompton Road to do some shopping. She stepped into Burberry to pick up a new trench coat and scarf for herself and Mithush. After a quick run into Prada for a 6 ring key holder and chain wallet for her daughter, she decided to go to Harrods. After trying on dozens of different looks she decided on the Valentino trousers and lace blouse, 3 dresses and the classic Balmain blazer with gold buttons. She boarded the escalator to Shoe Heaven while her sales associate Beatrice stored her bags. When she arrived on the footwear floor, she decided to start in the Manolo Blahnik boutique. She picked up a fresh pair of Hangisi pumps in black satin to wear with her new trousers. She walked through a few more boutiques until something caught her eye. Savannah stood in the mirror trying on a pair of Guiseppe Zanotti Claudia sandals when she heard a familiar voice. When she turned around she was surprised to see Ms. shoe addict herself, Brooke Taylor. Savannah let out a low scream and an excited Brooke ran up to her as they embraced. They hadn't seen each other in years and hadn't done well keeping in touch. After a few minutes, they found themselves in tears. Both women dearly missed Milla and were survivors of an elite sisterhood called reality television. The two women made it out unscathed but the majority of their peers hadn't. They decided to head downstairs to Ladurée for brunch. Savannah shook her head when she saw Brooke's haul; 14 pairs of Gianvitto Rossi shoes. "How many Brooke" asked Savannah. "At last count, it was 365" said Brooke. "One for each day! That's actually not bad" Savannah kidded. "Exactly!" exclaimed Brooke. "I only buy quality footwear so I'll have them for ages" Brooke added. As the ladies waited on their Croque-monsieurs and fruit salads they reminisced about Milla. Each woman had only known her a short time but they loved her to life. They gossiped about Morgan and Malcolm being in the news, Sydney's suicide attempt and Kent and Linda's accident. Savannah showed Brooke pictures of Leslie and Lloyd's wedding and children. During lunch Savannah learned that Brooke was in town with her husband. His name was Arrington Thompson and he was a restauranteur and master chef. In addition to his restaurant locations in Dallas, Seattle and Washington D.C., he was also a partner in a local food preparation service back home in The States. The delivery service sold healthy meals to people on the go. Brooke met him through her friend Nia's husband. They've been married for seven years and have a blended family. She told Savannah she knew it was possible to have a functional blended family, while watching her eldest son fit into his stepmother's family. Once a month her husband and children have dinner with her eldest son's father and wife's families. "Sometimes we take up an entire section of the Cheesecake Factory" giggled Brooke. Savannah smiled as she listened. It was a beautiful thing hearing about exes and new spouses getting along and being included by each other's families.Savannah brought Brooke up to speed on her new life in London. She told her about new properties that Mithush had acquired through her expertise. They shared pictures of their children and hilarious stories of motherhood. They laughed for hours and decided to shop some more. Before leaving the café, they bought boxes of Ladurée's famous macaroons. Later that evening, the two women parted but agreed to stay in touch.

Chapter 6: The Fullness of Time

JUDY sat at bible study laughing out loud. It had been several years since Joe gave her an ultimatum. When Judy expressed her desire to get back together, Joe told Judy he could no longer be married to an unsaved woman. After months of being offended, Judy had her come to Jesus moment. Morgan struggled in the hospital for weeks after catching the flu and seemed to grow worse and worse. Judy cried out to God and made a vow. "God if you spare my daughter's life, I'll live for you." Later that evening Morgan's prognosis greatly improved. When Morgan was released from the hospital and back to her routine, Judy disregarded her vow. One night around 3:06am Judy had a visitation that shook her to the core. Years later she is still unable to discuss the details. Needless to say, she surrendered her life to Christ and never looked back. She and Joe remarried in their pastor's office 18 months later after intense counseling. Morgan still lives at home and continues to struggle with her illness. Her condition is a daily reminder of the power of prayer and the cost of living a godless life.

Malcolm received probation for assaulting Morgan to nobody's surprise. He had to attend anger management classes and donate money to a domestic violence organization. Though he wasn't convicted of a crime he was exposed for his deeds. One of his women contracted the virus and told the entire world. She told everyone who would listen how Malcolm Ross gave her HIV. Though he'd infected half a dozen women, the others weren't willing to go public. Morgan declined the opportunity to make a statement and avoided the media's calls. Weeks later it was confirmed and he was forced to live his life in seclusion. To escape the public eye he moved to an undisclosed location and faded from the celebrity social scene. Three years later Malcolm was shot and paralyzed when the brother of one of the women he infected recognized him at a Florida saloon where he was working as a bartender.

Sydney sat in her cell writing a letter to Trixie. Tears fell from her eyes as she outlined the details of her life. So many women had been released during her sentence and it hurt to see them leave. Everyone who was incarcerated when she arrived were all gone except Khadijah. It was year 10 and it wasn't getting any easier. Her daughter Jill was 18 and Richie was 14. Jillian kept her posted but it wasn't the same. Jill was on her way to college and Sydney had missed her entire life. The fame, glitz and glam weren't worth the price. She still had nightmares about Milla and was awake most nights. Khadijah had her faith to keep her grounded but Sydney struggled to find God. She knew at year 14 Khadijah would be released because she was just 4 years away from completing her twenty year sentence. During a conversation with Khadijah she realized that her friend was already in prison while she was stuck in a trailer in Tulsa doing double shifts at Ruby's Diner. Jill was only 2 and Sydney hated her life. What she wouldn't do to get a do over. She wished it was possible to correct her mistakes like

Matthew McConaughey in The Devil's Advocate. At the very least she wouldn't have called Taylor. If she could go back even further she would've stayed in high school and finished. So often people are enticed by the idea of another life instead of working hard to change the life they've been given. Sydney had earned a degree in accounting during her sentence but it would be decades before she could put it to use. Khadijah told her to stay on top of new practices and certifications so her degree wouldn't be obsolete. Khadijah earned a certification as an herbalist and wanted to help people heal from natural remedies. Since earning her certification, she helped Samantha get rid of her acne and because of Khadijah's concoctions, one of the guards no longer has asthma. Since the corrections officer became asthma free, he sneaks in chicken boxes for Khadijah once a month. Each second Thursday she becomes excited like a kid in a toy store, waiting for her secret package. It was her guilty pleasure since she wasn't supposed to eat foods that aren't halal. In prison, everyone fixed their focus on something that would keep them mentally stable; For Sydney, it was Family Feud. She watched it daily and would play along with the contestants. She tried reading the dictionary like one of her tier mates only to learn it wasn't her thing. Khadijah had read over 600 books and loved to read. She was a wealth of knowledge and loved to educate her fellow inmates. Sydney loved to hear Khadijah speak. After starting out on rocky terrain they'd become good friends.

Year 11

Sydney is overwhelmed when she lays eyes on Jill for the first time since she was a toddler. The college freshman visits her mom for healing from rejection and abandonment. During their visit, Jill sees first-hand how unprepared Sydney is for life and motherhood. She finds empathy for the woman she spent her formative years despising and forgives Sydney for not being in her life. Before leaving, Jill teaches her mother about the power of the gospel. Sydney feels unworthy of forgiveness and rejects Jill's offer of salvation.

Year 12

Sydney continued to sit at Khadijah's feet and learned her black history. She had dropped out of school long ago but was sharp enough to remember that Khadijah taught her things that were never taught in school. She confided in Khadijah that the average Caucasian person has no idea what blacks in America have truly suffered. She also admitted that the opinions they have about blacks weren't based on personal experience. Khadijah began to see some things from Sydney's perspective and realized that someone of Sydney's pedigree wasn't the cause of her plight. The two prison mates called a truce and decided to expound on what was common between them.

Year 13

A rough year to say the least. Sydney dreaded Khadijah's departure and was petrified about being alone. She realized after all she had been through, she was only at the half way mark. Sydney spent months on the verge of tears and had several panic attacks. She was placed on anxiety meds and needed them to make it through the day. The sounds, smells and tastes of prison life got the best of

Convicted

Sydney begins watching new television dramas and hardly attends service. What's the point of continuing to attend if she doesn't roll on the floor and shout? She begins to stay in her cell and avoids participating in the activities she once found pleasure doing. Her insomnia returned and she grew restless. As her release date grew closer it seemed as though time moved slower.

Year 20

It was the week of Pastor Angie's release and the entire block was sad. Because Sydney enjoyed her teachings she decided to attend. Pastor Angie had given them so much hope and belief in themselves that they couldn't imagine how they'd make it without her. Many of the inmates expressed their desire to attend her new church when they were released and others hated to see her go. She reminded the ladies that they had One greater than her living on the inside of them. "My job is to show you Jesus not Angie" she said. "If you fall apart after I leave then I've failed you". A new inmate named Deja rallied the women and encouraged them. "Let's stick together and make Pastor Ang proud! Let's become who we were meant to be before the foundations of the world" Deja said excitedly. Angie's heart melted. The ladies began to sing worship songs and prepare for service. That afternoon Pastor Angie taught on condemnation versus conviction. "All of us may be convicted in more ways than one but the good news is with Christ we aren't condemned" she spoke. Sydney listened intently to the message and then it happened! She grasped a revelation of who God is! She jumped up excitedly for the first time. "I get it Pastor Ang, I get it!" Sydney yelled. Everyone was floored because they'd watched Sydney sit in her seat while everyone else shouted for years. Sydney's new found understanding sent the service to another level as the Holy Ghost entered their praise. During the altar call Sydney Marie Kane from Tulsa, Oklahoma accepted Jesus Christ as her Savior and was filled with the Spirit of God. That night she slept like a new born baby and woke up with joy in her soul. During breakfast, she learned about Pastor Angie's release. Though Sydney and her sisters were sad to see her leave they were ignited. Deja and Sydney learned how to pray and began to start prayer projects. Women would give them prayer requests and the two ladies would intercede. By the end of the year their intercessory group grew into 16 women. She began to pen pal with Joe Abal and accepted his forgiveness.

Year 21

Joe visits Sydney and encourages her to continue leaning on the Lord. He was shocked by his ability to sit across from the woman who ended his daughter's life without trying to strangle her. Now older and wiser Sydney made certain to apologize to Joe face to face and express her remorse for her actions all those years ago. Joe's forgiveness lit a fire inside of Sydney that made it necessary for her to do God's work.

Year 22

Sydney continues to labor in prayer on behalf of her fellow inmates. She learned so much about pain in the past twenty plus years. The private things she was told during prayer requests made her wonder if there was any good in the world. Still she was hopeful to dedicate what was left of her life to glorify God. She began to study the scriptures and couldn't believe how many movies and television shows had stolen its stories.

Year 23

Testimonies were rolling in and miracles were breaking out. Since the prayer team assembled, 22 inmates charged with lesser crimes had been released early. A few of them had their sentences cut in half. Not only did Pastor Angie write the ladies but Sydney became one of her mentees. Sydney tithed to Pastor Angie's church from an account she forgot she had. The tithe was enough money for the church to buy a small building and convert it into a beautiful sanctuary. Pastor Angie named the church Winepress House of Faith, after Sydney's favorite story in the scriptures. After years of seeing breakthrough in the lives of others, Sydney continued to believe that Richie would return to God. Jillian told her about his DUIs and drug abuse. Larry wasn't a good example and influenced him in error. Still Sydney prayed, fasted and made disciples out of those around her.

Year 24

While reading her monthly letter from Pastor Angie, Sydney was overwhelmed by her desire to ordain Sydney as an Evangelist. Sydney had grown in her walk with God and felt an unshakeable urge to tell everyone about Christ but she didn't realize it had a name. She looked forward to pounding the pavement on behalf of the Savior no matter what she was called. The praise reports continued to roll in and the intercessors continued to rejoice.

Year 25

On a frigid Monday morning in November, Evangelist Sydney Marie Kane was released from prison at the age of 52. Unlike her entrance there were no paparazzi or angry mobs. A generation had passed since her infamy was relevant. Society was more ensnared and dark than it was when she entered but Sydney had become a beacon. There to greet her at the gate was Pastor Angie, her husband Leon and Deaconess Tiona "Trixi" Brunson. After visiting with Jillian and the family, Jill agreed to work on establishing a relationship with her mom. They all agreed to pray for Richie and just believe. Sydney returned to Maryland and served under Pastor Angie. She had her breast implants removed and accepted who she was. The auburn hair she once dyed black now needed to be dyed auburn due to greys. Prison had aged her well beyond her years but Sydney was happy to be free. She became a part of the intercessory team and acclimated to life on the outside. Winepress was in Anne Arundel County so she found an apartment in Hanover.

Sydney quickly gained momentum in ministry because she hit the streets to spread the good news. She wasn't an itinerant speaker, she was a real deal evangelist plowing outside the four walls of the church. It wasn't long before she caught the attention of Christian programming and she made her rounds on all the relevant talk shows. She even reunited with Joe and together they traveled and taught the message of forgiveness. After traveling to 72 countries sharing her testimony and winning souls for Christ, Sydney's life changed forever. She had seen blind eyes open, deaf ears hear and 7 people raised from the dead. She saw limbs grow back, the terminally ill healed and people of other faiths embrace Jesus Christ. Without stepping one foot behind a pulpit, Sydney impacted the world for the kingdom of God. It had been a long process full of mountain peaks and deep valleys but Sydney had found her purpose.

...

The continual flow of rain drops splashing on Richie's forehead, brought him back into consciousness. As his eyes began to focus, he identified his surroundings. He was laying on Larry's living room floor directly under the leak in the ceiling. He quickly recognized the stench of his own bodily fluids and had no idea how long he'd been on the floor. Richie had gone on a drug and alcohol binge on Friday night. It was now Tuesday morning and Richie was yet alive. Sometime around Saturday evening he overdosed but Richie has two praying mothers. Both women felt the urgency to pray for him at the very time he was slipping away. Warring on his behalf, they won his deliverance in the spirit.

When Richie sat up, the television turned on, as if on cue. In awe, he watched an interview Sydney and Joe had done four years prior. He couldn't believe his eyes and ears as his birth mother shared her testimony of conviction. The scales began to fall from Richie's eyes while the presence of God filled the room. Crying out for his restoration, Richie vowed to live for God and return to his faith. Waves of God's glory transformed him from the inside out. It was as if time stopped just for him while he soaked in the majesty of Christ. Deep within his soul Richie found the grace to forgive Sydney just as Joe had. For the first time in years the Spirit of God gave him the utterance to pray with other tongues. From that very day, Richie was set free from drugs and alcohol and returned to his family. Armed with his testimony he began a successful program for addiction recovery. He met and married Katie, a kindergarten teacher who bore two children Jasper and Holly. Both children and their cousins Chad and Charles are the loves of Sydney's life.